Sanjay Sharma is a former badminton champion who represented India in the sport internationally from 1975 to 1990. He was appointed as the captain of the Indian team for the 1989 Asian Championship and 1990 Commonwealth Games and later served as the national coach from 1998 to 2003. He has won a record 19 Maharashtra state championship titles. He has also been a feature writer with numerous sports magazines and leading newspapers and was Chief Hindi commentator in Star Sports from 1992 till 1997 in Hong Kong. Later on, till 2018, he continued to commentate on international badminton events. He became a wheelchair user after being hit by Cavernoma of the spinal cord in 2020. This book has been very important to him as he tried to find out just why people with disabilities are not treated so well in the country and also how they can be brought up to do their might for society and work as equal partners in the progress of the country. He is the author of five books.

The Power of Divyang
by Sanjay Sharma
Paperback Edition

First Published in 2023 in India by

Inkfeathers Publishing
Vivek Vihar, New Delhi 110095
www.inkfeathers.com

Reading Community Partners

ISBN 978-81-19483-10-5

THE POWER OF DIVYANG

SANJAY SHARMA

Inkfeathers Publishing
www.inkfeathers.com

DISCLAIMER

This work of fiction, titled "The Power of Divyang", is a product of the author's imagination and creativity. While the majority of the content within this book is purely fictional, some elements draw inspiration from the author's personal life experiences and observations. Certain events, scenes, and aspects of the narrative might reflect aspects of the author's reality, but they have been woven into the fictional storyline for artistic purposes.

The book may also feature characters with names resembling those of real individuals, including the author's friends and acquaintances. However, any resemblance to actual people, living or deceased, is purely coincidental and unintentional. The author has taken creative liberties in developing these characters to suit the narrative's fictional context.

It is important to note that the political, controversial, and societal scenarios depicted in the book, including references to government officials, political parties, and related institutions, are entirely products of the author's imagination. They do not represent any real events, entities, or persons, and should not be interpreted as such.

The author has woven into the narrative a focus on the

challenges faced by people with disabilities in India. Through the creation of a fictional world, the book explores the potential of people with disabilities when they seize agency over their circumstances. While rooted in themes pertinent to real-life struggles, the story's unfolding is a product of the author's creativity.

Readers are encouraged to engage with the story as a work of fiction, appreciating the author's storytelling abilities while understanding that any semblance between fictional elements and reality is coincidental. The book's aim is to entertain and provoke thought, and any unintentional connections to actual events or individuals are purely incidental.

DEDICATED TO

This was a very difficult book that I have written. The subject made sure that I spilt my heart out. My very soul was laid bare for all to see.

Who do I dedicate this book to?

Well, firstly and most importantly, it has to be my wife and soul mate, Deepti. She has perhaps suffered more than me. Never leaving my side, she has been the epitome of decency and dignity in how she has dealt with the severe problems of being my caretaker. Her life has come to a standstill because I have to be looked after 24/7. I am able to survive basically because of her.

My two daughters, Medini and Shachi, have been exemplary in every way and have done their bit in looking after me.

My son-in-law Rikhil has been a pillar of strength. He is a caring, decent, honest, hard-working, forthright, focused, responsible, and respectful individual. The more I see of him, the more I like him.

Satya Prakash Tiwari, Rajaram Ghag, and Arvind Prabhoo have accepted their disability with bravery and are productive in every way. Their courage helped me understand my own disability.

Shaila and Shashi Welling the doctor couple who are very close to me. Despite his own severe medical problems, Shaila and Shashi have stood by me through thick and thin.

And finally, I dedicate this book to all the people with disabilities in the world.

May God give them the courage to face their trauma with patience and bravery. Not to leave out their caretakers and helpers whose life also becomes a nightmare.

SPECIAL NOTE

I have written about the problems that the divyangs have faced since independence. But today, things are changing, and the general society is more aware of the problems we face. The big change came after the 2020 Olympics held in 2021 in Japan due to the Covid pandemic. The non-disabled squad did not perform well at all and returned with very few medals. But the para-squad returned with a bucket full of medals. The nation went berserk, and the para-squad was felicitated right, left, and centre, including tea with the prime minister. The country saw this tea party with the divyangs, and is an eye-opener to society. The Government also did its bit by ensuring that the para-athletes got the same prize money as the non-disabled squad, and the sports ministry is now giving high-tech training and facilities to the para-athletes, levelling the playing field. I will not be surprised if the para-athletes again bring more laurels to the country as they did in Tokyo.

The sensation lasted for a long time. The nation was elated that our para-athletes had done so well. And this adulation has changed the mindset of the common man. People are becoming helpful generally, and I hope this continues so that the divyangs are respected and welcomed and become a part of nation-building. They deserve it.

FOREWORD

by Sandeep Singh Dhillon

As I eagerly flipped through the pages of "The Power of Divyang," I found myself transported back in time to my days as a badminton player under the mentorship of Sanjay Sharma, a man who played an instrumental role in shaping my career and my outlook. The short 156-page book begins by immersing readers in the glory days of Sanjay's sporting career, a time when he stood as an emblem of strength and tenacity on the badminton court, moving from representing India to coaching a new crop of players. As one of his proteges, I remember his passion for the sport and relentless pursuit of excellence. Giving up was never an option, especially for his students.

Little did we know that life had a different path in store for him, a path that would challenge him in unimaginable ways. The turning point in Sanjay's life came with a cruel twist of fate in January 2020 that left him grappling with a disability that profoundly altered his world. A cavernoma—cerebral cavernous malformation (CCM) or cavernous hemangioma in the spinal cord upended Sanjay's world, leaving him a wheelchair user. And with a new tag: disabled or divyang. Call it what you will; the result is the same. From taking care of his family, Sanjay needed taking care of, needing a support system. He writes about it in his usual matter-of-fact manner, putting the facts out there and sharing his struggles, both physical and emotional. His description of the physical and emotional pain Sanjay endured, and the subsequent transition from a non-disabled athlete to an individual who uses a wheelchair, is both heart-wrenching and inspiring. Sharma's vulnerability shines through as he recounts the difficulties faced by him and others with disabilities.

This is more than just a personal account; it touches on broader societal issues, particularly the plight of the "divyangs" (people with disabilities) and the barriers they face in an able-bodied world.

Hearing impaired myself, I have an insight into this world of people with disabilities. As a badminton player, I operated in a 'silent world'. Any player will tell you that aural clues help you anticipate your opponent's next move. The sound of the shuttle hitting the racquet, the sound of feet hitting the court, in doubles match communicating with your team player. I had none. But I learnt to compensate, adjust, and get on with the game of life, both on and off the court.

So did Sanjay. But this book is not about his struggle with his new 'wheelchaired-reality', but exploring the new world this new 'tag' led him into. A world ignored by those unaffected, and in India, largely ignored by the government and urban planning.

He writes about connecting with India's top para-athletes Satya Prakash Tiwari (Dhyanchand Lifetime Achievement Awardee) and Rajaram Ghag (paraplegic long-distance swimmer), and the legendary Arvind Prabhoo, a quadriplegic (chief trustee of the Prabodhankar Thackeray Swimming Complex) who let Sanjay into their 'Divyang' world and about turning disability into the power to conquer. Writes Sanjay of his encounter, "They have accepted their handicap with bravery and are productive in every way. Their courage helped me understand my own handicap."

Arvind Prabhoo's words underlined how far India still has to go to create an inclusive society for people with disabilities, "In America [unlike in India], they do not treat you as a person with disabilities. They just treat you as a person. You are treated the same as others. They have ramps everywhere, and all public transport is wheelchair-friendly." Not so in India.

Today with this book, Sanjay is a tireless advocate for the disabled community. He lays bare the lack, puts focus on the ham-handed facilities (for example, ramps that don't really help), public transport that leaves the disabled stranded, complete lack of access to government offices, and that's just the tip of the iceberg.

Through the pages of "The Power of Divyang," Sanjay takes readers on an introspective odyssey, offering a glimpse into the inner turmoil and the profound impact of such a life-altering event. His unwavering determination to come to terms with his new reality and his tireless efforts to adapt and find a new purpose in life left me in awe of his resilience.

One of the most poignant aspects of Sanjay's candid deep dive is an exploration of the broader societal issues surrounding disability. As a hearing-impaired individual, I have experienced firsthand the misunderstandings and prejudices that can exist within society. Through his words, Sanjay skilfully shines a light on the challenges faced by the disabled community, urging readers to reevaluate their perceptions and foster a more inclusive and compassionate world.

But there's a twist in the tale; a third of the way through the book, Sanjay imagines what the future could be if this innate resilience of the 'Divyang' were harnessed to force change. What if the disabled community created a platform to showcase their collective strength and flex their political muscle as a lobby, a vote bank? This 'future', as Sanjay sees it, could be the way forward. Saying more about the plot and this fictional future now would be a spoiler.

But as he narrates his tale at breakneck speed, it is like watching Sanjay on the court, smashing his way through to a nail-biting match-point finish.

As I journeyed through the pages of "The Power of Divyang," I couldn't help but feel a profound sense of gratitude for having had the opportunity to be coached by Sanjay Sir. This book is a compelling narrative that not only urges us all to reflect on our own biases and perceptions of disability but opens our minds to the possibilities of what can be achieved if the 'power' is harnessed. This book is a true celebration of the power that lies within each one of us to overcome adversity, embrace diversity, and create a more inclusive world for all. It need not be a fictional future anymore.

Sandeep Singh Dhillon works in ONGC as Chief Manager

ONE

Present

It was a mesmerizing scene at the Haji Ali Dargah traffic square, which handles probably the heaviest road traffic in Mumbai, was suddenly inundated in a most astonishing manner by some citizens with disabilities, in a wheelchair, people with visual impairment with the most recognised walking cane, supported by the deaf people, people in callipers or on crutches, few double amputees who dragged themselves furiously and so on. They were protesting against government policies that had entrapped them in a life of trauma and isolation.

This was a well thought strategy intended to show the power of the divyang to the state government. The intention was to bring the headstrong government down on its knees.

These people with disabilities then occupied the road coming into the South Mumbai area and the road which took the traffic back to Worli and beyond.

One group locked the road coming from Tardeo to the suburbs and the road going to Mahalaxmi, the local railway station. In short, the traffic was totally paralysed; they also had brought with them thick ropes which were connecting all the protestors in such a way that they became one unit and not individual units of 25-30, so that it became almost impossible for the police to catch them.

One group had done the same thing on the western express highway where traffic coming into the city and going past the toll *naka* (plaza) at the Sea Link from Bandra to Worli, and from Sea Link going out to the western suburbs.

Borivali station was also targeted in the same way.

This was also done at 11 a.m., in a real synchronised manner and with the precision that would shame an army commander. And another group at the Shivaji Chhatrapati Maharaj Terminus, or CSMT as it is known. An extremely busy junction, it was the headquarters of the Central Railway for both the local and up-country trains. It was estimated that 2 lakh cars use this area daily.

The chosen junctions and traffic squares saw, in all probability, the heaviest and busiest traffic in the city. By 11:30, there was utter chaos in the financial capital of the country. People got stuck and were cursing and screaming at the local police in general and the traffic department in particular.

Many people stuck in the traffic wanted to go to urinate but could not go leaving their cars. So, letting it out on the pavement was the only solution. Dear reader, this became the main news on that day. Not just local news, but it had caught attention world-wide. The media, including BBC. CNN, Fox news, Al Jazeera, etc., were rushing to join reporters in the area.

So why did it happen, and what was my role in the entire scheme? After all, I was just a very fit badminton player for India. We will see later on why this blocking of traffic occurred. Why did I go through this even though I knew that I was committing a grave crime?

Now see my history and my background and read my story.

I am a wheelchair user. And I am not at all happy about this. In fact, I hate every minute that I am in a wheelchair. But it is very ironic that the wheelchair also gave me a kind of status with enough power to bring a state government down to its knee. Don't believe it, keep reading, and you will know. Also, read my personal story on how this came about, returning to where I left off.

A combination of a few devastating factors hit me very badly in 2020, making me, like others in my type of situation, a burden on society and one on their family. My family consists of my wife, Deepti, my elder daughter Medini and the younger one, Shachi. My father expired in 2010, and my mother, a Covid victim, breathed her last in 2021; under harsh rules and regulations due to the pandemic, no more than seven people could be part of the funeral rituals.

So, each of these three women in my life has a very strong personality. They most brilliantly took charge of one aspect of my personality, ensuring that the family remained financially strong and well-knit and that I never felt a lack of anything. Yet the thing was so shocking that each of us withdrew, in a cocoon, wondering what had hit us. How was life going to change? Will I be able to recover from this ordeal, or will I be handicapped for the rest of my life?

My Sports Addiction

Everyone who had known me or had heard of me and followed my career could not believe how a physically strong and fit person like me could be laid low despite leading such an illustrious career. So, allow me to present forthwith glimpses of my career. With great pride and to the point of being immodest, let me confess here that I used to be one of the fittest sportsmen in the country during the time that I represented India in world badminton.

I played for India for a good 16 years. That is why it was not easy to accept that I would be a wheelchair user, that I would one day not walk at all, I would be so sick, a super fit person like me. Even at 63, I was the epitome of fitness, tough and trim, with a personality that stood out. At least, I thought so. I had a punishing schedule as far as physical fitness was concerned.

This demanding physical training schedule helped me nicely as I turned out to play for the National veteran championship in 2013 and 2014 and won the doubles titles in the 55 to 60 age group. I was a multiple national titles winner.

I had never been inside a hospital, going there only to visit a friend or a relative. I had not fallen sick at any time in my life, barring the common cold, which was basically due to my dust allergy and a low fever at times, attributed to sheer exhaustion. So, what had gone wrong so drastically that I landed in a wheelchair, a certified person with a disability? That comes a bit later. Right now, I want to discuss how I remained so fit.

Given below is a glimpse of my training regimen during a typical week.

The 16 years saw me playing 8 All England championships, often the Malaysian, Indonesian, Thailand, Singapore, Hong Kong, and China Open. More importantly, I played 4 Asian Championships in 1983, 1985, 1987 and 1989.

The biggest feather in my cap, however, was the 1979 Asian zone Thomas Cup finals, where we defeated hosts and holders Malaysia in Kuala Lumpur, and reached the event's final stages, essentially the Men's World Team Championships. I played in 4 Thomas cups in 1979,1982,1984, and 1986. In the 1979 edition of the Thomas cup, playing the first doubles with my partner Pradeep Gandhe, we created history by defeating the then world number 2 pair of Kwek Choo Peng and Ho Khim Soon in two straight games with contemptuous and facile ease.

I say contemptuous ease as the local media had written us off, saying to play against their terrifyingly aggressive pair was like leading lambs to slaughter. We gave everything in that match to cock a snook at the local media. I also played in the Commonwealth Games of 1990 in Auckland, New Zealand. But the glory beyond my dreams was when I was appointed Captain of the Indian squad for the 1990 Commonwealth Games and the 1989 Asian Championships.

It is correctly said that to reach the peak is easy, but to remain there on top for many years is extremely difficult. That I remained on top for 16 years speaks volumes about my basic fitness. To give you an idea of my training schedule for an average and typical week, allow me to reproduce here what it takes to reach supreme fitness levels, which could help you dominate your sport.

Monday mornings, you would see me pounding the pavement for a killing 12 km run. Since I live in Mumbai, the citizens here will understand what a 'killing' run I am referring to. From the PJ Hindu Gymkhana on Marine Drive, I ran to Nariman Point, back again and to Chowpatty, up Malabar Hill to Teen Batti, full Ridge Road down Kemps Corner to Babulnath Mandir, back on Marine Drive, and then finished at Hindu Gymkhana. It was a solid run, and in the last 400 metres, so we sprinted. Mind you, I had the company of other top shuttlers, which was always pleasant and welcoming.

Back at the gym, a light breakfast and stretching, a small break of 30 minutes, and off to pump iron for an hour at least. After weight training, it was stroke practice for one hour, some drills on the court trying to cut down wrong techniques so that I did not make any mistakes during matches. Then smash practice, basically hammering the bird as fast and as much power as you could generate. I would finish all the above by 11 a.m. Go home for rest and a good lunch. I would return to the gym by 3:45 pm to play at least 5 or 6 blistering games and finish the day at 6 pm.

Tuesdays were short sprint days. It was a combination of 25 metres, 50 metres, and 75 metres. It would entail 4 or 5 sessions of 25 minutes each, and every session left you exhausted. I took a 10-minute break after every session.

It was back to the badminton court for some killing shuttle runs and stroke practice before signing off for the morning part of the day. The evening was all-out games, as usual.

Wednesdays were the primary skipping day. It was a 90-minute affair with a lot of fast skips and lots of double skips. After a short break, it was 60 minutes of pumping iron with intense work, lighter weights, with many fast repetitions. From 4-5 pm, I was only attacking badminton drills of both singles and doubles as I played both events with Elan—followed by defensive drills for 60 minutes. Some days, at least twice weekly, I would play three sessions. Why? Let me explain this.

Glutton For Hard Work

Some days I played or trained vigorously three sessions a day, going all out and putting my last ounce of energy into the game. And two sessions came within an hour of each other to put that extra pressure on me. I could play two hard matches within an hour during any tournament. Since I played both singles and doubles, this happened quite often. The afternoon session could be anything from court drills to shadow badminton exercises, lasting anywhere between 60 to 90 minutes.

Thursdays saw deadly uphill runs. At the end of a 60-minute session, I was utterly exhausted. Again, a Mumbai resident would know how hard it is to run up the 150 metres stretch to Mount Mary Church in Bandra, adjacent to superstar Shah Rukh Khan's Mannat. After this arduous run, my group would jog down 5 km to our special cutting chai adda. Lots of stretching was done as the chai was being brewed. Then we had freshly baked sweet biscuits from a bakery near the *chaiwala* (tea vendor) that rounded up the morning session. The evening session was not held as the body was allowed to recuperate.

Being involved in sports from the time I played in Nagpur from age 12. Also, because I used to write about the game extensively, covering many tournaments for newspapers, I had always watched the news on TV. The 2016 Olympic Games I watched very keenly following the progress of our badminton queen PV Sindhu who smashed her way to the finals, only to lose out to Spanish sensation Carolina Marin after leading match point on two occasions.

She got the silver which was a first for India.

But on return to India, when a big group of athletes came down from the plane, there was a huge reception as Sindhu came into view. There were a couple of para-athletes also returning from Rio with medals, including the female athlete, who got a silver medal, but no one at the airport welcomed her.

Friday mornings, fresh from the rest I had on Thursday evening, I eagerly hit the weights gym for circuit training, a combination of light weights, yogic stretching, high knees, tapping, star jumps, kangaroo jumps, etc. Evenings were as usual, but one versus two games where you played alone against two opponents; this helps improve speed on the court.

Saturday, in my opinion, was the deadliest. I had to do a combination of 100, 200, 300, and 400 metres sprints this day. Each had to be run with total effort; one has to be satisfied that one has done his best. There was no fooling anybody. You answered your own conscience. I can say that I died after each session; such was my intensity during training. For these 100, 200, 300 and 400 combinations, I did 6 to 8 repetitions—60 minutes of weight training followed by a brief rest. The evening was games practice, as usual.

This schedule was not followed during tournament times, when one had to go fresh and rested, looking forward to playing your best in every match.

Sundays were fun days. Just relax and enjoy yourself with anything you want. Catch up with sleep, catch up with friends, family, etc.

There, dear reader, you can see how fit I must have been. There was not an inch of unnecessary fat on my body. I followed this punishing schedule for almost 18 years, keeping me near the top of the pile in Indian badminton, and helping me to remain in the Indian squad for 16 beautiful years. I was ranked India number 1 in doubles and number 3 in singles. I had a fast sizzling playing style in singles which accounted for victories over all other Indian players. Still, against the mystifying genius of Prakash Padukone, and the sheer doggedness and controlled stroke play of the late Syed Modi, I crumpled as I could not penetrate their defence.

Prakash was the world's number 1, and Syed, at his peak, was no. 12 ranked. It was an honour to play the third singles for India in the Thomas Cup of 1984 and 1986. Apart from the 1979 Thomas Cup, I gave India another solid victory in the 1984 Asian zone Thomas Cup event in Delhi's fabulous Indira Gandhi Stadium.

Playing against Thailand in the third singles, I stepped onto the court after Prakash and Syed had won their singles in hard-fought matches. I looked at my short but stocky, well-built opponent Vichiytra Aswanapakas, who was ranked much higher than me in world rankings (Why the Thailand people have tongue twisters for names is beyond me, but I can vouch for the fact that the Thai people are amiable and well mannered.) He looked tough and experienced, but I had the advantage of a good 6-7 inches on him in height, and more importantly, I was playing at home, in front of my people.

I had a simple strategy to catch him napping; push him to the baseline with low flat services and fast speed tosses, which ensured the net area was beyond his reach. I kept plugging away with full body line smashes, sharp, fast drops or half smashes played with a wrist-snapping stroke. He was unnerved when I reached a good early lead of 6-0 in the first game. After that, it was a massacre, and I stumped him 15-3/15-2. The Hindustan Times the next day wrote, "Though there were players like Padukone and Syed Modi in the squad, it was Sanjay Sharma who played the best match for India."

Mind you, there were no air-conditioned courts in my time. Playing in such courts is far more accessible in closed courts with hundreds of spectators; with all windows and doors closed, the court is like a boiling cauldron. After every game, you have to change your shirt.

Furthermore, badminton in those years was played on a 15-point-score line but with service changeovers. Points were scored on your service and not on rallies, as it is today. This meant that the matches were far longer in that era. I remember playing a doubles match which lasted 1 hour and 32 minutes. I lost more than a kilo of body weight.

And from so many matches I had played for India, if I have to pick up another scintillating match, it has to be my classic encounter with Stephen Baddeley in an India versus England test match at Gloucestershire, UK; this was a 5 test badminton series. Stephen was the English national champion and also ranked number 2 in Europe. In earlier test matches, he had defeated Syed Modi and Partho Ganguly. Our coach TPS Puri asked if I could play him in our last test; I said I would love to play him. I had defeated Stephen before while living in the UK for my studies. It was in an inter-county match. I knew how to tackle him, and I beat him 15-7/15-8.

TWO

Making Waves Internationally

You must have had a glimpse of what I was all about—my doggedness, competitiveness, and achievement in attaining super fitness. My being a player who relished and raised the bar when representing India in team matches. And now, as a person with a disability or a disabled man, whichever way you call me, it is something I would never have dreamt would happen to me in my most nightmarish of dreams. I heard demeaning words like *bechara* (helpless fellow) or *is ki to zindagi kharab ho gayi* (his life is ruined) hurled at me in undertones that invoked my anger, but what could I do about it?

One moment I was as strong as Dara Singh, and the next, I was helpless, a man who could not even tie his shoelaces; this is a real sorry state I find myself in. I have to be helped by a 24/7 helper, I can't walk at all, and the most demeaning thing is that I can't attend my ablutions without the helper present. And if he is on leave, my wife or even my daughter Medini would attend. It was highly embarrassing.

I was a solid 6-footer with rippling muscles and a fit, trim person from whom emanated that lovely fragrance of total self-confidence. A real fighter on the court, I never gave away my matches without putting in my hundred per cent. I played not to win but to satisfy myself that I had done my best. It is a very important factor in a player's character and psyche.

So, what had happened to me to make me use a wheelchair? What had made me so ill that my world spun down an abyss from which there seemed no return? After I announced retirement from competitive badminton in 1992 while still being a state champion, fans asked me again and again why I retired while still being a Maharashtra state champion. After all, my partner Uday Pawar and I defeated the current India pair of Rajeev Bagga and Bhushan Akut.

While they were both around 25 years of age, I had crossed 36. Again, my fitness had been tested, and I had won.

My dream run in life came to a ghastly end on the night of 16 January and the morning of 17 January 2020. I had a meeting and returned home from Dombivli, some fifty kilometres away, where I had met the officials of Lodha Builders, who wanted to start a badminton coaching academy. The meeting was good, and they wanted me to give a proposal. I was well known as a serious coach in the city, and Lodha had done research before zeroing in on me as soon as possible.

After I announced my retirement, I went into coaching with zeal. I had three centres running, and I had a great time nurturing the talent of tomorrow. I started coaching much earlier; between 1982 and 1989, I produced 7 national champions in junior age groups. Later, I was appointed national coach between 1998 and 2003. I have, to date, coached and mentored some 37 national champions. I had the pleasure of coaching such illustrious names as Pullela Gopichand, Jwala Gutta, Chetan Anand, Rajiv Bagga, and Sandeep Dhillon in national training camps. In those years, it was mandatory for the team travelling abroad for international matches to undergo rigorous training in camp before departure.

Bagga and Dhillon went on to bag the Arjuna award. My first national champion was Amol Shah in 1982, and my last was Simran Singhi in 2015.

Coming back from Dombivli, I was dragging my right foot, which my wife noticed immediately. "What is wrong with your right leg? You are dragging it. Are you feeling alright"? Nothing wrong with me; I told her my lower back was having some ache. I feel it more as I bend down to pick up the shuttle. I have sprained it while coaching, I guess. I am going to sleep so don't wait for me for dinner. I will be alright by morning."

The fact was that I had been having pain in my back for some months, I attributed it to some young kid trying to run me out of the court as defeating "Sanjay Sir" was something to relish. So, I must have overstretched somewhere, and I always thought these slight pain here and there was a gift for playing sports. It was the '*meetha dard* (satisfying pain)' we liked but ignored willingly.

At about midnight, I got up to relieve myself, but moving my legs gave me immense pain. I called out to Deepti. She was alarmed seeing my face, which was sweating. She tried to help me get to the toilet, but I hit the floor with a large thudding sound. as we approached the urinal door It was as if my legs had been cut off. She yelled for Medini, Shachi and Rikhil, my son-in-law (Shachi's husband); they ran out to see what the commotion was about.

I was sprawled on the floor. Rikhil is a big man; he effortlessly picked me up and waited till I relieved myself with the help of Deepti. It was way past midnight, so the family huddled around and decided to take me to the emergency ward of the Ambani hospital at around 8 am; at about 6 in the morning, I wanted to go to the urinal again but did not want to disturb Deepti.

I started the journey with some trepidation while stretching out my body to take support from the cabinets. When she suddenly woke up and saw me stretched like Spiderman, she shouted for help again, and the three kids came, running in to see the problem. Rikhil picked me up, and Deepti helped me to relieve myself. Almost shrieking because of my excruciating pain, I came to the bed on the side closer to the bathroom. Just before I could ease myself into the bed, I fell with a thud, screaming for help, and started crying. "That is it. We have to take him to Ambani right now," yelled Deepti. And that is how I landed up in the Ambani Hospital, close to my house.

THREE

Present and Past

I was forced to accept the fate that had befallen me.

I was really an extrovert and a fun-loving guy who played hard and partied harder. But once I became a person with disabilities, a divyang, all this came crashing down. I tried to understand the problems people with disabilities face and how they may affect me. The idea to show the power of the divyangs once they united was basically to ensure that these people also should have a life. Their own idea of fun and frolic rather than biding time till your number comes up in the computer of Yamraj.

I thought of the idea of the Divyang Unnati Sangthan, or DUS, to give us a base and an identity. This is the beauty of real Democracy. It looks after the very downtrodden and weak.

And we did not intend to hurt the citizens with our traffic blockade. It was basically to ensure that they think about us, to open their eyes to the trauma we faced every moment of our lives. The power of the divyang had to be respected. Let's see now how I reached that stage. For that, I will have to take you back to my arrival at the hospital.

At the emergency ward, a cluster of junior doctors surrounded me, wanting to see and hear from me and Deepti what was wrong with me. On the surface, I looked alright, though the insides were in turmoil. I had never been in this sort of situation before. The director of Neurology, Dr. Bhatt, arrived and went into a huddle with his team along with the neurosurgeon Dr. Abhay Kumar who concluded that I had no brain stroke or paralysis. What then was wrong with me, as I could not find any sensation in my legs? CT Scan and MRI were undertaken, and finally, I heard the dreaded name of CAVERNOMA in hushed tones. Surgery will be required.

The neurosurgeon Dr. Abhay came to my bedside, called for Deepti, and with a serious look and even graver voice, told us that the matter was serious and that after seeing the results from various tests and scans undertaken by me, he and the neuro team strongly felt that Cavernoma had struck me and also Dr. Abhay Kumar described Cavernoma like this, "A cavernoma is a cluster of abnormal blood vessels, usually found in the spinal cord or the brain. Also called 'Cavernous angiomas', a typical cavernoma looks like a raspberry. Mount Sinai Hospital in the USA says, 'The cavernoma can range in size from microscopic up to several inches in diameter.'

Interestingly, one in 200 persons has cavernoma from birth, but it mainly stays docile and benign. But it can cause seizures, stroke, haemorrhages, etc. Most people never know they have one. But if the lesions burst and bleed in the brain, it can cause neurologic problems and even death. So, what triggers this deadly problem? The experts you meet will tell you, "There is no clear reason why a person develops a cavernoma. Nothing to say that it is inherited or if there is a genetic disorder. Cavernomas occur randomly."

So, there it is, in black and white; I had been chosen randomly to be hit in my spinal cord. I don't smoke, I am a highly regulated social drinker and have no doping or drugs, so why I was chosen thus by the Almighty is something only he knows. I was just a victim in his scheme of things.

One truth I understood after this episode is that you can be as fit as anything. Still, you simply do not know what is happening inside your body. I hear so many cases where cancer victims come to know about when it is in stage three or even four. Can you imagine international sports icons like Lance Armstrong in cycle racing, Martina Navratilova in Tennis, and our own Yuvraj Singh in cricket, never knowing about cancer they nurtured inside their super-fit bodies? After regular exercise, diet control, and staying away from alcohol, tobacco, controlled sweets, and oil in food, you can ensure that you look fit and younger for your age.

But the truth is that the outer *'chamak dhamak'* (shine and glitter) cannot control the insides of your body. So, obesity, BP, hypertension, to a great extent, diabetes, cholesterol, and maybe a couple of other problems will not occur if you lead a disciplined lifestyle. But things like Cancer, Brain stroke, Cavernoma, Parkinson's disease, Alzheimer, Epilepsy, etc., you will never know till they establish themselves deeply in your body.

The operation was critical and had to be performed; too much delay could be fatal. Dr. Abhay had another problem. My issue was one in a million types of problems. The Cavernoma is mainly the bunching up of blood vessels, but they stick to the outer wall of the spinal cord. It is easier to go inside with the help of a laser and simply pluck the cavernoma and pull it out. But in my case, it was bunching and growing inside of the cord, where the surgery has to be very delicate and requires a very seasoned surgeon with ice-cold veins. Dr. Abhay was such a surgeon.

He told my wife upfront that the surgery was critical, but he gave a 70% success rate in surgeries of such kind. "Madam, I must tell you there is a chance of slicing the wrong nerve, which will be catastrophic. So, we have to be careful. But surgery is the only option. So, we need your consent immediately."

The consent was given, and I went under the knife for this delicate procedure for the first time. This procedure lasted almost 4 hours. The 4 days in the ICU after the surgery went without any problems as I was heavily drugged with steroids. I do not recall the ICU as I was in and out of a stupor.

Nevertheless, in the ward, I was aware of what was going on. Dr. Abhay took two rounds and started to take extra care. He and his team had learned of my status as a sportsman. And yes, somehow, they also knew I had authored two books, the first one called Pullela Gopichand—the World Beneath His Feet. And the second one is called Courage Beyond Compare; both books did well in the market and were appreciated.

Nevertheless, this is straying from this storyline. Dear reader, we can discuss this in some other forum. But now, let me tell you how doctors, in hushed tones, were discussing how my life would be in a wheelchair from now. No one was telling me anything, but I could gather from whispered sentences here and there that my future would not be rosy.

On the 10th day in the ward, Dr. Abhay came on his rounds and could see that the depleted strength from my legs would not return in a hurry. My left leg had no strength, while my right one could muster up only 25%. And I could not move even one toe in my legs. Alarmingly, I could not feel any sensation in my legs. My wife walked in, looking as radiant as ever, and Dr. Abhay beckoned her to a corner where the whispering began.

FOUR

Chicken Legs

"Madam, I am afraid he may not be able to walk again. The trauma he has suffered is very deep. We have done our best. He must undergo physiotherapy to strengthen his muscles; it is the only way out. Otherwise, he has to use a wheelchair; this will be a long journey. He is a reputed sportsman and may overcome these problems with determination."

Deepti is made of steel. "Doctor, he will walk one day and soon. We are not people who give up easily. He never gave up on badminton courts and will not give up here; this is a challenge we will face together as a family," she said.

I had heard that I would have to use a wheelchair for mobility. The very thought was deafening and terrible. I could not think of myself being in a wheelchair. I was still in the hospital and started having dark thoughts about my future and myself, and I cried, cried, and cried in my loneliness till no more tears came down from my swollen and hurting eyes.

Furthermore, I was also having incontinence, an aftermath of the spinal operation; this means I had no sensation for bowel movement or when urine was to be passed. My body was a wreck. During the 43 days that I was incarcerated in the hospital, my muscles had atrophied to such a state that the kid from the adjoining room, whose father was admitted because of a serious cardiac problem, whispered to me very innocently, "Uncle, uncle, you have chicken legs," and then clucking like a hen ran around the room, till his startled mother, with an apology written all over her face, caught hold of him and hauled him out of the room. However, I wondered what he meant by chicken legs. Since I had been flat on my back for days, I was in the hospital, and I could not see my legs; such was my physical state.

In any case, I had no sensation in my legs. When the nurses came to give me a sponge bath early the next morning, I requested them to bring a mirror and place it on such an angle that I could see my legs. I was aghast and stunned to see them in the mirror. These were not the legs I remembered I had. My legs were chiselled and muscular, strong and powerful, my pride and it had taken years of toil and a punishing training schedule to make them look good.

What I was looking at was two chopsticks, bereft of any muscle. The calves and hamstrings had no flesh on them. When I started walking, I cried at what I had lost and wondered if these two legs could carry my weight. That kid had been right. I had chicken legs.

Money is Everything

I could not imagine myself in a wheelchair with a urine bag in front of me. The very thought was revolting. This picture, however, stuck in my mind, and I was afraid that this was the reality of my future. I had nowhere to go and no place or person to turn to except the welcoming embrace of my wife. She tried her best to console me; my daughters' smiles warmed the cockles of my heart, but dark thoughts made a house on one side of my brain, and they visited me leisurely.

How would I sustain the lifestyle my family was used to? If I could not move or walk, let alone run with the kids who wanted to get fit, why would they take coaching from me? All my three centres would not be able to work in my absence. I could not blame the parents who started withdrawing their children from the coaching after that honeymoon period of two weeks when they all would say how sorry and sad they were to see me in a wheelchair. It was just not me, they would say, and after making vague promises of being in touch, they would say goodbye, and all will move on. How could I blame them?

The only earning member with a steady job in my family was my elder daughter Medini. Deepti was a housemaker, terrific at that. Shachi was a young filmmaker, still to find a foothold in the Bollywood scheme of things. In short, though we lived well, we were in real trouble if my coaching money was cut off at the source, not a *paisa* coming in. Although she had volunteered to pay for all household expenses, I did not like that idea.

Every father has a responsibility towards his family. After all, you have brought the children into this world, and because of you, your pretty wife was uprooted from her parents' home, from her comfortable surroundings, and thrust into a very unknown and alien world, surrounded by people not known to her; you have to ensure that they are well looked after.

Nevertheless, one lesson from my suffering is that you must save enough to ensure you can pay your medical bills because you never know when you will be a victim of severe health issues like I was.

Not only you but also the family depends on you for this. People will say, just to comfort you, that money is not everything, don't listen to them. Believe me, money is everything, or damn close to it. I was lucky that I had such a strong sports background.

I have spent a huge amount, almost ₹70 lakhs, on my illness. I will spend almost 50,000-60,000 rupees monthly on physio, helper, medicines, etc., for the rest of my life. To this end, I am very grateful to the Mumbai Badminton Association, Maharashtra Badminton Association, and the Badminton Association of India, who heard my appeal and sanctioned ₹11 lakhs between them towards my medical assistance.

Sunil Gavaskar, my old friend and a legend with a golden heart as chief trustee of Champs Foundation, sanctioned almost ₹10 lakhs, and that Motley Group of Veteran Shuttlers calling themselves 'Badminton 45' got me ₹10 lakhs as well. I realised that I had a lot of goodwill in the badminton scene in India. I must have delighted all above with my style of play and a never-say-die attitude on the court.

A Bitter Experience

Anyways right now, I must add here that it is essential that you get medical insurance, something like a medical claim. Hospital charges, doctors' fees, medicines, etc., are high. It will break your back. I must say that my medical insurance saved me from going bankrupt.

I must confess that when the ads started coming out for medical insurance some 30/35 years ago, I was very sceptical of their success. I avoided getting involved, even though many people told me it was helpful. I ignored all these suggestions at my peril, at the cost of my foolishness.

My father was a cancer survivor. He was diagnosed with lymphoma sarcoma of the limb in 1953, just six months after marrying my mother. He lost his left leg in a marathon operation under the watchful eyes of Dr. Jussawala, the famous oncologist, in

1955 at the Tata Memorial Hospital in Mumbai. He learned to walk on crutches, which he used throughout his life. He was a very senior central government officer. He retired as Principal Accountant General in Maharashtra. On his retirement, he was appointed director of many loss-making companies to help them enter the black.

He was to travel to Ahmedabad to attend an AGM of one such company when he fell from our 2nd floor apartment at Juhu, tumbling down the staircase and landing on the turnaround between the 1st and 2nd floor. He broke his elbow, wrist, and ribs. He had to be taken to the emergency room of Nanavati Hospital, where he was not admitted until around 10 pm. Whatever cash I had, coming to roughly 5,000 rupees, was insufficient to cover the deposit demanded. And mind you, the debit cards and ATMs had not reached even the preliminary levels of science fiction; the human mind had not thought of such scientific extravaganza yet; and yes, we had no medical insurance. No banks were open after 3.30 pm, so no cash could be withdrawn.

We were in a fix, and if it had not been for financial help from some friends in our society building and a few relatives living nearby, my father would have died because of loss of blood.

It was one bitter and harrowing experience I had. You can, of course, guess what prompt action I took the next morning. Yes, dead right. I got everyone insured in a hurry. As for me, I survived what could have been a major heart attack. I almost fainted when the hospital bill was presented to me. Total of ₹85,000—took my breath away. Even after deducting this, that, and the figures mentioned in the small prints, the insurance company would have shelled out about ₹68,000. I could have lived with the balance of ₹17,000 payable to the hospital bill.

FIVE

Tryst With Cancer—A Life Lost

I am digressing again, but please bear with me. All I want to tell you is that don't make the mistake I made or Ramesh did. It will help you tremendously if you have taken out medical insurance. I did not take it, and neither did Ramesh. We both suffered.

Because not caring about yourself and indulging in habits that can cause cancer, you are playing with fire. You can also become a person with disabilities, a divyang for life.

A good worker, Ramesh, was in my department at a company I used to work for as VP of facility management. I saw him eating tobacco and told him to quit this bad habit, but he just smiled and said nothing. I forgot all about this for three months until I saw him eating tobacco and trying to hide the sachet as he saw me. I gave him a piece of my mind. Furthermore, he also flouted the company rule of no cigarette and no tobacco policy by eating tobacco on the office premises. The government of Maharashtra had also announced a complete and blanket ban on *gutkha* (tobacco) and related products.

I called him to my cabin and explained how tobacco chewing could lead to mouth cancer. Nothing will happen. "Sir," he said, "I do not swallow the *gutka* but throw it out after some time. Nothing will happen to me." It was a typical way of explanation by a tobacco addict.

Suddenly, it came to my mind to ask him about medical insurance. "Do you have medical insurance? For you and your family?" I asked. "What is that for? I have some insurance done by employers. In case I die while in service, my family gets ₹5 lakhs. That is all I need," he said, indicating that he was late for work and had to leave. That is standard corporate insurance issued for each employee when they join. I told him that we would talk about medical insurance.

Ramesh was typical of the youngsters from UP and Bihar who made a beeline to Mumbai to get jobs. In their home states, there were hardly any jobs available. There was no future. Farming was the only option. However, when the internet reached the innermost life of the villages, the youngsters got exposed to the outside world. It was exciting and colourful, waiting to be explored.

The farms were getting smaller and smaller as a family was getting bigger and bigger. So, Mumbai, where the construction business was almost always booming, was the big magnet attracting young men from the hinterlands. Such boys like Ramesh, who has a couple of sisters to marry off, a younger brother who was in school, and perhaps a mother who was alive, was a typical story of many young men wanting to find their footing in the world. He was responsible, so a good part of his salary was sent to his village. The two-acre farm that the family had was barely sufficient to produce enough for the family. A part of the produce from the farm also found its way to the local *mandi* (market), where they got enough money to pay a monthly tuition fee for Ramesh's brother and medicine for the old woman.

Typically, of the way that Indian social life worked, the son had to be given the best possible that a family could afford. *Paraya*

Dhan (another's money/liability) was what the girls in the family were called. Since they were in the house only until marriage, they were their husband's responsibility. So, why shower the girls with the best that the family could afford? Ramesh's sisters had to leave school and learn household work, as the mother-in-law expect that.

Ramesh was a happy and soft-spoken youngster. He was dutiful and worked hard. Did not have any bad habits except enjoying a smoke now and then. He knew what he was doing was not good for his health, but he could not stop it. Like all other young boys, he had also picked up the habit because of curiosity and, of course, encouraged to smoke by a senior resident of the village. He used to see two or three persons going through the village on bicycles and throwing glowing cigarettes butts on the ground. One day, he ran after them, and that was it. He picked up the almost-finished piece and did not give it up till now.

Ramesh had lost his father when he was 18 years old. Working late at night on their small farm, the father was bitten by a poisonous snake and died almost instantly.

Ramesh had to take the responsibility of earning and running the family now. Money was always short. A friend told him about opportunities in Mumbai, and he decided to try his luck as early as he could. He did various jobs, learnt to drive, and after two years of working here and there, landed in my facility management department in my company.

Another few months passed before I came across Ramakant Patil, the transport department manager, where Ramesh was transferred from my department. I casually asked him the whereabouts of Ramesh. Patil knew that I had sometimes used the services of Ramesh when I had meetings with clients. In addition, I admired the driving skills of the man. Patil, however, looked at me quizzically. "You don't know?" "Know what?" I asked, sounding somewhat perplexed.

"He died two weeks back; cancer killed him. He was diagnosed with the third stage of the deadly disease. Cancer of the mouth—he found some painful ulcers but did not pay heed. When it became unbearable, he went to Tata Memorial Hospital, where the doctor took just one look and told him; the ulcers were small, black, and malignant tumours. Per the company's regulations, his mother and family are coming in a few days to collect the insurance pay-out of ₹5 lakhs."

I was too shocked to react, and I bid Patil goodbye and decided to meet the clients. But my day was already spoiled. My head started throbbing, and I decided to go home and sleep it off. In the next few days, I learned more about what had happened. His family had come down to the streets. To pay for the treatment in Mumbai, they had to sell off the farm, the brother could not pay school fees, so he was out of the school. What the old mother will do with two unmarried daughters is anyone's guess. To say that Ramesh was obstinate and stubborn was an understatement. He had laughed at my suggestion that he take out medical insurance. That proved fatal at the end of the treatment he underwent.

He survived for only three months after he had been diagnosed with third-stage cancer. In the last three months that he underwent treatment, he had been billed ₹12 lakhs. Plus, change for his treatment at the hospital, which was highly subsidised. The family was devastated. If only he had taken the insurance as I suggested, the family would not have suffered so much. So, dear reader, take heed of what I say and insure yourself and your family. You will sleep with ease—believe me.

SIX

Why Do I Hate the Wheelchair?

We have digressed enough from my main storyline. Let us get back to it. Why do I hate it when I am in a wheelchair?

I hate being in a wheelchair. For the simple reason that it is a sign that advertises you are helpless. In my case, the disability is complete. The combination of three deadly things, Parkinson, Cavernoma, and the left hip transplants that had been put in after my fall in the bathroom when I fractured the hip, have devastated my and my family's life.

A slight bulge in the area created balancing problems as I started to tilt slightly toward the right when I sat down or walked with a walker. In short, until this book was written, the balance problem remained acute. And yes, before I forget, the aftermath of the operation also saw my left hip lose a centimetre in length; this meant the left shoe's sole had to be increased by a centimetre. It looks okay but creates problems while walking. But I have a problem.

The combination of the three factors I mentioned above has created untold complications, problems, and misery in my life; I can't bend down to wear shoes, I can't wear clothes unless helped, I can't stand without toppling over; in short, I am immobile, and I need a helper 24/7. I cannot do anything myself. I am dependent on others to do the simplest of tasks. I have no control over my body. I have no control over my bladder. I was on a catheter for 3 and a half years. So, I always had to wear a urine bag, which I hated.

I am helpless. And here is where the problems begin. Indians have not been very friendly or helpful towards people with disabilities. As a society, we have failed people with disabilities in their quest to find level playing fields—helping them unleash their true potential. Though change is happening, I feel the man on the street has more empathy towards people with disabilities. He comes forward to help them always.

How do foreign countries, especially Western democracies, treat their disabled citizens?

Treatment of People with Disabilities in India and Abroad

When my father was transferred to the Indian High Commission in London, I also went along with my parents. I carry many memories from my early days in England, and one of the most acute ones I have is from the Wimbledon Tennis championships and the All England Badminton Championships played at Wembley.

The first is tennis, which I was lucky enough to see on a Rover ticket, which meant walking only. On a Rover, one could walk to any court except the centre court, but you could not sit down as no seat was allotted to you. Moreover, to get a Rover, you had to queue in front of the ticket window. You had to queue all night to have a serious chance of getting a ticket, but it was fun as many of us brought breakfast, tea, coffee, and snacks. It was a picnic sort of atmosphere, thoroughly enjoyable.

One day at the quarterfinal stage of Wimbledon, I saw a green coloured bus arrive with 10 wheelchair users. The driver and the two attendants were in green military uniforms. The bus was wheeled to the VVIP parking area. A ramp-like structure came out of the back of the bus, and one after the other, the wheelchair users came down, ushered by the young soldiers. There used to be a small terrace on court one, and all were taken there to watch the matches. I was amazed at what I saw and on enquiry I found out that the club did not charge people with disabilities a penny and were not only here to see the matches free of the ticket price but also provided snacks, tea, coffee, etc., treated as guests of the club. Mind you, this was way back in 1975.

I saw the same scene when I played my first All-England Championship at the Wembley arena in 1975. I was very happy for this disabled group as well. I asked my neighbour in Wembley, where we lived, and he said that people with disabilities are part of the general society and must be helped however they want. This is our duty.

Not only this, but I also saw toilets for people with disabilities everywhere—none in India.

However, I forgot about all this as a struggling youth. Terms like disability did not exist in my dictionary and were far from my mind.

Then in 2014, I released my book 'Courage Beyond Compare'. The same year, I was selected to represent India in the Veterans' World Championship in Istanbul. I was more aware of the needs of people with disabilities because of the book I had authored.

I was really happy to see ramps, toilets, and special facilities everywhere for special people. In India, these facilities were missing. Not only this but their public transport system was also geared to meet the demands of people with disabilities. Every bus had an automatic ramp slithered down to allow wheelchairs to go up or out.

There was nothing of this sort in India. I realised this when I became a person with disabilities. My first tryst with the problem of being such a person came when I went to register a power of attorney I was giving to my brother-in-law. This government building had no ramp. One had to negotiate 6 steps before catching the lift from the landing, which took you to the registrar's second-floor office, which was very cramped. The lift was so small that one had to be a Houdini to get into it with your helper.

We had almost turned back knowing all this when a watchman from an adjacent building approached us to see if we wanted any help going to the registrar's office and said that if we agreed to pay ₹100, he and his colleague would lift me along with the wheelchair to the lift and will also bring me down on our return. It was a brilliant *dhandha* (business) for him as he confessed to being asked how many wheelchair-using patrons visited the registrations office daily. He said roughly 10-12 wheelchair-using persons came daily, meaning a neat ₹1,000 daily at least, to add to his kitty. At least someone benefits from the misery of people with disabilities, I thought.

Later on, after 1990, I have not travelled much, but during my playing days, I visited 80% of countries in Europe and Asia. All countries of Europe were very aware of the problems faced by people with disabilities and bent over backwards to make their lives easier. But not so much in Asia, where like India, the treatment of people with disabilities had left much to be desired.

Divyangs are a Sizeable Number of the Population

So, where in India do you find satisfactory facilities for people with disabilities? Practically nowhere, I am sorry to say. Suppose you compare it with all developed countries in the world. How many wheelchair users do you find on the street? Come on, be truthful, dear reader. None, I would say, unless you are standing in front of a hospital or front of a temple or a mosque.

The roads of Mumbai are so bad and full of potholes of various sizes and depths that even craters on the moon must envy them; besides, the traffic is so unruly and dense that no wheelchair user can even attempt to negotiate them. You rarely see wheelchair users in government buildings, public buses, railways, cinema halls, beaches, inside temples, and sports meets unless it is for athletes with disabilities.

Even in banks, for their financial transactions, you will not find wheelchair users. I can go on and on. It is as if people with disabilities have no right to entertain themselves. They have no right to 'life'; people with disabilities are forced to live isolated lives. We are a neglected lot. However, what surprises me is that with 7 to 8% of Indians classified as physically disabled, the governments, down the ages, right from 1947, had not done anything concrete to help. People with disabilities are not just polio survivors, amputees, Parkinson's and survivors of Alzheimer's and advance dementia survivors, dwarfs, but also people with visual impairment and deaf people; they are also disabled.

I interviewed Devendra Jhajharia, the most honoured para-athlete in the country; he has two Olympic gold medals in one arm javelin throw, records in the World Para-Championship, and Asian and Commonwealth Games. He had featured in a chapter in my book 'Courage Beyond Compare'. This legend said to me in Jaipur, where we had met, that my statistics of 7-8% of the population as people with disabilities was way off the mark.

"Sir, anyone over 75 years of age is also disabled. They have problems with their eyes, ears, knees, hips, etc. The government says these senior citizens are 13-14% of the population. So, I believe some 19-20% of Indians at any given point are people with disabilities." This was an eye-opener for me. There are so many issues for people with disabilities that need to be resolved.

The main ones to be started at war footing are:

- All public transport, like trains and buses, must be wheelchair-user-friendly; this means enough space for climbing in and going out. Things are changing in the country but really slowly.
- All public buildings must have ramps everywhere and elevators where required. The Government must pass this order with immediate effect.
- All government and private companies and business houses must have reservations of up to 10% of the workforce. The percentage can be staggered. People with disabilities will get a lot of self-esteem if they start earning. It will also ease the burden on their families to a good extent.
- People with disabilities or workers with disabilities must get a tax break. Their medicines, physiotherapy, doctors, and hospital visits are for life. If you ask me, there should be no tax on their incomes.
- As mentioned above, special hospitals should be dedicated to people with disabilities so they are not forced to stand in queues. If they are confined to the bed, then the government-approved medicos must visit them at home.

In comparison, let's see how America treats its people with disabilities. Arvind Prabhoo, chief trustee of the Prabodhankar

Thackeray Swimming Complex at Parle-East in Mumbai. "I never felt that I was a person with disability when I was in America for 6 months after my accident in Bangalore."

SEVEN

Arvind Prabhoo, the Superman

Arvind is quadriplegic; he has no sensation below the neck but is an extraordinary personality. He suffered a nasty accident when he was just 20 years old. His father was a doctor, and so was his mother. His father was also the Mayor of Mumbai and a local MLA. When he saw his son, he realised Arvind had to go abroad for treatment as his injuries were deep. The family zeroed in on a hospital in America where he underwent treatment.

Still, finally, this hospital could not find any cure. Arvind was destined to be a quadriplegic. Yet he never took help from anyone, including his parents, to stand up in life. It is incredible to know that it is this man who brought cable TV to India, formed a company called Orbit TV, and sold it to Zee TV for a good profit. It was then named City Cable.

A real philanthropist, he took over the role as Patron of the Indian Women's Cricket team for 6 years, funding them to play all over the cricketing world, and in the Women's World Cup of 2005, he saw to it that India reaches the finals. He also got Sahara India to give a sponsorship of 1 Crore to the Indian Women's team, a huge amount in those years. And yes, he was instrumental in bringing in Mandira Bedi as the brand ambassador of his squad.

His love for sports was not limited to cricket. At the time of writing this book, he is the Founder- President of the Pickle Ball Association of India as well as the President of the Mumbai Suburban Table Tennis association.

In America, he spent his time socializing, finding new friends, and simply enjoying life in America till he had to return home. "You know, in America, they do not treat you as a disabled person. They just treat you as a person. That's it. It did not matter to them if you came in a fancy car or by a wheelchair or even if you walked in. You were treated the same as others. They have ramps everywhere, and all public transport is wheelchair-friendly. I used to go to pubs very often, and every pub I went to, had a couple of high tables which accommodated wheelchairs. Every restaurant I went to, had the same. You had complete access to libraries, sports stadiums, cinema theatres, and what have you. You are not singled out. Society is very inclusive, and no one judges you. In Boston, where I was situated, and elsewhere I saw how the people with disabilities were treated."

Arvind said, "The most fascinating thing was how people with disabilities got involved in social rehab and got along with society." In India at that time, the people with disabilities were considered a curse from god, as if they had brought this problem upon themselves."

In America, society never discriminated against people with disabilities. Since all are treated equally in the same way, it gives you much confidence. People will not say or even hint that "*Arre is bechare ka kya bhavishya hai? Use dekho kis tarah baitha hai. Bechara seedha bhi nahin baith sakta. Is ne kuch pap kiya hoga pichale janam mein. Is ke karma kharab hain. Is par shani ka bhav hai.* (What future does this helpless fellow hold? Look at the way he is sitting! He can't even sit straight; he must have sinned in his previous life; his karma is bad; his stars have a fault)."

Arvind has a dynamic personality; despite his disability, he has lived vigorously. In my last book, 'Glory Beyond Dreams', he says that in the Boston hospital where he had gone for treatment, Arvind had told his parents that, since it was now clear he would be quadriplegic all his life, he would like to chart his course. He would not like to be a burden on them or a burden on society. Once the financial burden becomes clearer, families become agitated slowly as the expenses of the disabled family member eat into the house budget.

Especially a paralysed patient like me, says Arvind, who is paralyzed neck under, as I mentioned before. It is an expensive proposition even to keep them alive. Moreover, apart from the family's burden, many mental, physical, psychological, and social issues and changes occur. Since the patient cannot travel, the family has to forego family functions; even if they went, one family member had to stay home as the caretaker. Resentment, thus brewed, under the surface and simmered to explode one day against the patient. And it is natural that slowly, the younger ones in the family, who are looking for a career to be made, find less and less time to spend with you. Others in the family slowly drift away, leaving you to your own devices. You become irrelevant. So, it is very important that the family stays with you and is willing to look after you, come what may. They must be committed to you and love you to the bottom of their hearts. Arvind's family was one such, and so is mine. I will forever be grateful and indebted to them for sacrificing their lives and well-being for me.

Family Means Everything

At the head of this extraordinary endeavour is my wife, Deepti. A multi-tasker par excellence, she took over most of the hard work required. Before my illness knocked me down, she was not very outgoing, but she came into her own and took over my role in my absence. Before this, I was around to do all the outdoor work, including all banking work. After all, as head of the family, the finance was under me to ensure that the family lacked nothing.

Deepti has not missed one session of mine with the physio, not even one consultation with the doctors; she was there every day in the hospital where I was incarcerated for 43 days. Most importantly, she concealed her emotions remarkably in front of me. Always smiling and cheerful, Deepti never shed tears when I was around. All the grief and sadness were bottled up inside to be felt when she was alone. She is more than my wife. She is my life.

What can I say about, Medini, my elder daughter? A real go-getter, she took the onus of all outside work, including ensuring that groceries were always available. The salaries of the household staff were paid on time, but much more than this, she, along with her mother, took over the nurse's duty. When my Urethra catheter was removed after 3 years, the urologist told us I had to use a condom catheter. I also had a long, troubling bed sore, which required dressing twice daily.

Deepti did that nicely as Medini took over installing a condom catheter without inhibitions. "Don't worry, Dad, I am a grown-up girl now, and you don't have to feel embarrassed. We can't go to the hospital every night to put on this catheter. I don't feel bad about this." She said, understanding my reluctance to see she was putting on the condom catheter.

Furthermore, she bathed me when the helper was not around. She had a full-time job with Star Sports but juggled her job and my need and requirements like an expert juggler. A very strong person physically, Medini is a former Tennis international. She has broad shoulders on which I lean a lot, especially when down and depressed.

In February last year, my younger daughter Shachi shifted to Canada with her husband, Rikhil. She is smart, a great communicator, good with investments, and is the finance minister of the family. She pays all bills and juggles all investments to get the best returns. She is very emotional and cries whenever she knows I am not well. She talks to us twice daily. Her smile and lilting laughter make my day.

The family, therefore, is the key to any person with a disability. Without the unwavering support of the family, it isn't easy to survive. I also abhorred and disliked the word used in context to anyone; 'not normal', but to describe a *bechara* or *lawaris* (heirless) is spoken to indicate having physical problems and helplessness. No doubt things are changing in the country, which are positive changes, but these changes, if any, have sailed past me. It is very ironic that out of all the people in this world, I get hit by such circumstances and become wheelchair user.

My book 'Courage Beyond Compare', highlighted the extraordinary achievements of our disabled or para-athletes who overcame disability and adversity to become champions. It was also an attempt to highlight the neglect of this segment of society by our brethren, who will never understand the trauma faced by people with disabilities every minute of their life.

Little did I know after a few years of writing that book, I would be disabled. Today, I face the same severe problems I saw in persons with disabilities, but I remain neutral in my opinions. Afterall, I had watched disability from a very close distance, as my father, about whom I have written in earlier chapters, was majorly disabled. I was, therefore, not overly sympathetic to their cause or feelings.

Nevertheless, here I am, riding on the same horse. After undergoing immense problems myself, I truly understood my dark future. Though, my wife and Medini always indulge me, taking me out for drives on weekends and giving their shoulders to cry on when I am feeling really low and depressed, I know it cannot be forever as they have to lead their own lives. Medini has a very demanding job with weird timings.

Yes, I cry a lot, as I get emotional on many issues. And I don't think that crying is for sissies. I feel that one must let out their emotions. Do not keep it coiled inside of you. Crying is a very natural phenomenon—no need to curb it. Be yourself.

EIGHT

Satya Prakash Tiwari

So, how do people with disabilities in our country face the problems, and how do they overcome these issues? Let us see what two veterans, iconic para-athletes who have won great laurels for the country in the international arena, have to say about the problems they faced in life and how they overcame such issues.

Satya Prakash Tiwari, or Satya as he is called, had the horror and mortification of having both legs amputated as he faced a future full of life and death issues after slipping and falling on a moving local train in Mumbai. He was only 16 years old at that time. His dreams of becoming the next Gavaskar were shattered, and so was the fallback option of joining the military. He adored Sunil Gavaskar and often sneaked out of the house to catch him batting in some international event. His father did not like Satya wasting time watching some cricket matches or others on TV owned by the neighbour. However, cricket was a magnet whose pull Satya could not ignore.

Like any other teenager, he was also fascinated by the men in uniform wanting to guard the country's borders. With hardly a future to discuss, he somehow walked into para-sports and found his calling. In a glittering career in para-athletics, he won numerous titles and medals in domestic events and 16 international medals, which included a gold in the Wheelchair Badminton World Championships. He knows the negative conditions that persons with disabilities face and problems that must be addressed with priority.

It is horrible conditions that we face day in and day out. Normal people will never understand the trauma we face. The simplest of things that can help people with disabilities to lead a better life is denied to us. We got independence in 1947, but our problems have remained unattended. So many governments have come and gone, but no one has ever bothered about us. We pay taxes like any able person but do not get any benefits. Clearly, Satya is agitated and worked up. He was venting the anger simmering inside his mind and body for many years.

I asked him what are the basic problems faced by people with disabilities. "Sir, there are so many that it is difficult to choose which one to start with; but let us take the ramp problem. Most buildings in India don't have ramps, even new ones, despite an order from the supreme court, if I am correct, that all buildings must have ramps, and even if the ramp is there, it is very awkward, made by amateurs who don't understand the concept of ramps. They tend to give more height at the starting end of the ramp. How does a wheelchair negotiate this? And if two persons are required to lift and put him on the ramp, the very purpose of the ramp is defeated.

The answer is to get an expert to explain how the ramp should be made. In 1960 or 1970, a law passed that buildings up to 4 floors need no lift. Why? People with disabilities had to stay only on the ground floor? No one gave a thought to why this discrimination against us was made. I live on the first floor of such a building, and since I do not have legs, I have to crawl up and down to my flat like an animal. It is not a pleasant sight."

Satya was honoured in 2021 with the Dhyanchand Lifetime Achievement Award.

Continuing his rant against the system, Satya says, "To get inside a government office for your work is a nightmare. It normally has a very small lift where a wheelchair cannot enter. In any case, the lift is invariably some 4-6 steps up. So, I have to wait on the pavement, hoping some good Samaritans will come and carry me up the steps at least; this is very demeaning."

Rajaram Ghag

Rajaram Ghag is a phenomenon, a very rare kind of Indian. A paraplegic with no sensation below the waist, he excelled in swimming. Then he chose long-distance swimming as his sport to excel in. This is unusual because swimming is one sport where hands and legs both play their vital roles. Hands to propel forward and legs to give the required thrust. So, with his legs not supporting, why did he choose marathon swimming with normal people competing? He explains that he is patient and likes the solitude of long-distance swimming, where he can plot, plan, and strategise on his stamina and speed. Swimming for him is therapy. He looks frail below the waist, but the upper body is all muscle and steel. The biceps and triceps are rock solid, bulging, and so powerful that even Arnold Schwarzenegger would have envied them.

After competing in many long-distance swims, like the 74 km race in the Ganga river from Kolkata in Bengal, the 34 km swim from Dadar to Mulund, and the 36 km swim from Dharmatar to Mumbai, he was ready mentally and physically, to challenge one of the deadliest seas on the planet. In this treacherous English

Channel, four-story high waves can pommel you and pulverise you by throwing you around here and there.

Rajaram trod the path of the legends and wrote history on 22 August 1988 by becoming the first paraplegic in the world to do so. It was not a victory for him but a triumph for humankind. Rajaram was born with both legs joined together. His mother was shocked and started crying when she saw tiny Rajaram and did not want to handle him. She thought that God was punishing her for some bad deed she had committed. Rajaram says that he had to undergo 16 major surgeries, and by the time he turned 8 years old, he could finally walk with the help of callipers.

Rajaram feels that many persons with disabilities, including himself, have major anger toward society. Why I had to suffer was the main grouse. Why couldn't I run, play like other boys and lead a normal life? That anger festered like a wound inside of me. It has never left me. I am still angry. Why was I chosen to suffer? That simmering anger today finds problems with the facilities provided to people with disabilities. "The public transport system is pathetic. Forget the buses, as with wheelchairs; it is impossible to enter. The entrance is very narrow, and the steps are too steep.

Trains are another matter. I have travelled all over India, and trains are the favoured mode of transport. However, the journey is a nightmare and a torture. Firstly, we cannot climb up to the coach, as the three steps leading to them are steep. Neither can we help each other, as everyone in the group is disabled. Therefore, we must request fellow non-disabled passengers to help us by lifting us to the coach. Many a time, we are rejected. I hate to ask any person not in our group to help us. Once you are helped to reach your seat, other problems start. I call it the water-relieving time. If you want to urinate, if all 6 from our squad are in the compartment, then there is no problem, as we use disposable water bottles or urine collection bags to pee in and throw them outside.

However, if other passengers are in the compartment, there is a problem. It is a nightmare to go to the toilets, as they are very dirty and too small to take a wheelchair inside. Even people with disabilities using callipers find it too difficult to use the toilet. Dear reader, you cannot even begin to understand how horrible it must be for both legs amputees, for double amputees as they are called. They have to crawl through the compartment and toilet's dirt and slime. The choice for them is to degrade their body or not use the toilet and suffer.

So, what alternative do we have? We do not eat until the day before the journey. We starve ourselves. If the men somehow manage, the women with disabilities have a nightmare journey every time they travel.

This country has been manufacturing buses and trains for a long time, at least for the last 45 to 50 years, and yet have not understood the need of people with disabilities, or they and the government are least bothered about us. We can be ignored because, perhaps, we are not a vote bank. We are not a nuisance. Now and then, one reads in newspapers that so and so minister from so and so State is going to Europe to observe such a process and bring it to India to benefit our people. They spend crores on these jamborees, yet not one has seen it fit to save people with disabilities from misery. We do not count in the scheme of things of any government or agency. We have no voice, as no one represents us.

Even in the financial capital of India, you do not have public toilets for people with disabilities. These ministers who go out for observation cannot see how people with disabilities are treated abroad. What facilities are provided to them? Travelling inside Mumbai is a nightmare. Without accessible toilets for people with disabilities, we either pee in a disposable plastic bottle or just keep the urine in, which is harmful, according to doctors.

We, people with disabilities, cannot leave the house for a long time. What will happen if I need to urinate? What will happen if I need to use a toilet? We have no life. I used to wonder what these politicians and bureaucrats would do if they could not use the toilet for 8-9 hours.

*****

The great champion Rajaram says, "The train journey nightmare starts when you reach the station. Very few stations in India have slopes on one platform only. These slopes are too long sometimes, making it difficult for wheelchair users to use. You have to keep on waiting till some good soul wants to do a good deed and helps you climb the slope by pushing your wheelchair to the top and then down to the platform where your train is supposed to come. (But what if the platform designated for your incoming train suddenly changed?).

I once had this nightmare while waiting for my train at Mathura Junction. At the last moment, the platform was changed for some technical reason. There was a stampede as all waiting passengers began rushing to the platform announced. Surely, some did not make it. I was fit and young then, and only with one handbag I raced to the next platform and jumped into my compartment. I am sure that no senior citizen above 65 would have made it, and not any citizen with a disability."

Adds Satya Prakash, "There has been some action by the railways recently. One compartment is designated for divyangs, which is a good idea. But the problem is a gap from the platform to the train door. Furthermore, we are allotted some 10-12 berths, and many disabled categories and even non-disabled are supposed to use this facility. It includes pregnant women and cancer patients.

The problem is that many non-people with disabilities enter the compartment and occupy their seats. And the people with disabilities are vulnerable, while the railway authorities do not check if we are comfortable."

The problem for women in wheelchairs is so acute that they never venture outside the house for months. Just because accessible toilets for persons with disabilities do not exist, and even if they exist, they are filthy. It has been observed that the general public uses them at will. As told, this bleak scenario by these two icons made me angry.

There was more to come from these two stalwarts who have been disabled for decades. I knew that in our country, not much is done for people with disabilities. They have a miserable present with no change anticipated for the future, but what gets me angry is the attitude of our politicians and senior officers towards people with disabilities.

NINE

The above champions have missed national events if the train journey is long, mainly because of the toilet issue.

Imagine the plight of the paraplegic since most of them do not have any sensation below the waist. They train their bodies in such a way by following a schedule to use the toilets, which means that they will use the facility as per the timings they are used to. In crowded trains, it is very difficult to reach the toilet. And there is another problem for them. They have a helper travelling with them, and two people can't get inside the railway toilet, along with a wheelchair. Why can't government and the railway ministry get together and find a solution; rather than treating people with disabilities as if they are a sub-human species? Is there any technical reason?

Let them share it with us. But I have a solution for this, which I will discuss later.

Satya, being a double amputee, has a major problem. He has to crawl and drag himself to the toilet, carrying newspapers or plastic sheets to clean it before using it. Dear reader, just see and imagine this scene. You will have tears rolling down your cheeks. How can we torture and rob the dignity of our fellow Indians? Don't we have any conscience at all?

There is a simple solution to end this nonsense. Why can't the engineers who have designed the railways think of this if I, with my limited intelligence, could think? To make the toilets bigger, the railways must sacrifice 4 berths and use that extra space to make good, big, hygienic toilets. So, they will lose some revenue, that's it. The Railway Ministry will have to decide if they want more money or the comfort of the citizens.

Before we see the problems faced by us people with disabilities in aeroplanes, let me bring an anecdote here that this true-life incident happened with the para-queen of the eighties and nineties, Malathi Holla—first, some background on her. Malathi had been a complete para-athlete India had seen. Champions like her are born once in a century. In wheelchair racing, she was supreme and excelled at the Para-Asian Games and the World Para-championships, winning 30 international medals.

In the domestic scene, she was supreme for decades, dominating her event. A fiery and brave competitor, she started entering the men's event as there was no opposition to her in the women's races. And she started to win medals here, too. In my book 'Courage Beyond Compare', she was one of the featured 10 iconic para-athletes.

I write here two episodes that describe the no-nonsense attitude she had in 1988 she was selected to represent India at the Busan Asian para-games in Korea. Already late to get the visa, Malathi approached the then sports minister Margaret Alva, a well-known politician, to help her. Margaret Alva flung her papers back to her and said, "You think you are PT Usha? If she can't win medals in the Asian games, you think you can?"

Madam said, "PT Usha could not win 100 metres in wheelchair racing, and I cannot win the flat 100 metres like her. I am not her, and she is not me." Afflicted by a rare strain of polio, Malathi had her papers signed immediately by a stunned Alva. But we have digressed a bit. Just wanted to show you that Malathi is one hell of a gritty woman.

In 1994, she was appointed as Manager of the Syndicate Bank. Her home was far from her branch, and taking an autorickshaw to the office and back, was proving to be very expensive. Of course, climbing and travelling by public bus was out of the question. She found it difficult to travel. One day a colleague told her that the government had waived the ₹1,60,000 import duty on the purchase of a car by a differently abled citizen of India.

But the finance minister's office in Delhi would give the exemption documents. An elated Malathi went about planning her trip to the capital. She caught the train that would take her 46 hours to reach Delhi. Undaunted that she could not use the toilet for 46 hours. She looked forward to meeting a Member of Parliament (MP), from Bangalore, arranging the pass to allow her to enter the finance minister's office.

Upon arriving at the office, she and the MP climbed up the first floor to reach the office of Shri Manmohan Singh, the then-finance minister of India. He was sitting with Arjuna Singh, also a cabinet minister. Let me quote from my book 'Courage Beyond Compare'. "(Recalls Malathi—both the ministers were in a bad mood. Malathi showed her documents and certificates detailing the medals she had won internationally. But it looked as if both ministers were not impressed.

Dr Manmohan Singh asked her how can he believe that she was Malathi Holla and how can he believe these certificates were true, belonging to her." The iconic athlete retorted, "Excuse me, Sir, but how do I believe you are Dr Manmohan Singh?" An angry Singh asked her what she meant by her words. And Malathi simply told the two ministers, "Why would I come all the way here in a 46-hour horrific journey where she had to control her bladder, could not use the toilet, and face deep mental trauma, for what? Just to cheat the ministry?"

A stunned but smiling Dr. Singh said the central duty exemption papers would await her when she reached Bengaluru. And true to his words, the papers awaited her when she reached home. It was great because Malathi had opened the doors for other disabled persons to buy specially customised cars. All they had to do was to get the central duty exemption papers from Delhi. The story here is not just how this legend got the car duty waived but an athlete of India of her stature has to undergo such hardships. It is a shame for our country.

TEN

Coming back to our story, how do people with disabilities react to flying? The problems remain the same. Toilets are the main issue as the ones in the aeroplane are too cramped. You can't take your wheelchair inside the plane, as the planes have their own wheelchairs, which can fit inside. Says Rajaram, "Most of the airports have good and accessible toilets, clean and roomy. However, there is the problem of non-activity. It is not much of a complaint, but we are stuck to our seats. We also do not eat or drink much, which could lead to problems, especially on long flights."

How do our super champions compare India to other countries? "There is no comparison between India and abroad. It is not just a case of availability but also cleanliness. Not only do we see a lot of respect for people with disabilities, but also the facilities are all clean. You can enter every building there. There are ramps all over. Public buses are accessible, with the entry point of the bus being equivalent in height, or buses have lowered ramps for passengers' convenience. I still do not understand why we have so many problems and why we can't solve them?" frowns Satya. I wanted to confront one of these IAS wallahs in the ministries of urban development or transport or the Chief Ministers' office to discover why this callous attitude towards the citizens with disabilities was.

To make ramps or public toilets for people with disabilities or make public transport buses, and trains easy to get into, is no rocket science. It is common sense, but we, people with disabilities, have shown no inclination to confront the government. Living happily, enveloped in our vulnerability, on this issue. Most Indians have this '*chalta hai* (it's okay)' attitude. We are not at ease if we have to confront the authority on any issue. There is an inherent meekness in our genes. Perhaps it is because the Moghuls ruled and the British ruled for 700 years. We lost our identity and willingness to question or confront the rulers on any issue, including those against our grain, accepting it as our karma. Well, I am cut from a different piece of cloth. I am by nature a confrontationist—I confront authority wherever I feel they are acting against my interest. My entire life as a top-class badminton player is a testimony of the tough stand I took against the Badminton Association of Indian Officials, who wanted to ban me for life from playing the game simply because I used to write in media about the misdeeds of these officials. Writing in the press is my fundamental right, as enshrined in the constitution, and no one can deny this to me.

According to Rajaram, the government is doing much better than before. For example, public toilets are being built. Still, they are too few and far between, and there is no maintenance or security to ensure that only people with disabilities use them. The facility is soon used by the local *janta* (public) and not by those for whom it is meant to be. Things were bleak, and there seemed to be no respite from the problems faced by us disabled. Civil society was oblivious to our plight, or they felt they were not losing out on anything by ignoring it out of hand. So, with nothing good happening, people with disabilities were leading the same mundane life they were used to.

I have written about the financial and social pressures on the family if there is a disabled member who has to be looked after 24/7. Many families are shocked when the news comes about one member who has fallen extremely sick or had met with an accident or had a brain stroke or anything else that has hit him hard enough to be called handicapped or disabled. The family gathers around the patient, love and anxiety pouring all over, assuring him they are here, and he need not worry about his future. Everything seems hunky-dory at first, but not for long, as fissures appear in the bond that has glued the family together. I do not blame the family for this, as everyone has priorities that must be met, career aspirations that take priority over anything else, and their need for social attachments for their psychological well-being. The family slowly drifts apart, with the patient being left alone more often than not. In this scenario, no one can be blamed. It is just fate or destiny.

ELEVEN

Now very much part of the disabled family, I also had a taste of things to come. My younger daughter was first initially reluctant but soon showed enough courage and maturity to migrate to Canada with her husband, Rikhil. It was bound to happen. As in their film-making field, there seemed to be no future here.

In Canada, they landed jobs in filmmaking companies soon after they reached Vancouver. Of course, we were very sad to see them go. That lilting laughter of Shachi, that physical reassurance of Rikhil, the fights with Shachi when she was adamant about doing something that we were not happy with, to the experiments with cooking food during the lockdown. So many instances to remember them by; we were going to miss all this. As usual, I cried a lot but then reconciled and accepted the fact that children are like baby birds; they will fly the coup someday. Afterall, they have their future and lead their own lives. As someone told me about children, "*Aap bachon ke janma data hain, bhagya vidhata nahin* (you are the creator of your children, not the creator of their destiny)."

Medini, after wonderful work done at the ICC T20 World Cup in Australia for her employers Star Sports, was promoted, which meant much more responsibility on her shoulders. She tried balancing office work and house responsibilities and giving her parents enough time, but it did not happen often. Deepti and I were mostly on our own. Nonetheless, life had taken such a drastic turn for me that she also got dragged into the abyss where I was swimming in, for no fault of hers. I could not drive the car now.

Perpetually gone were the days we went on long drives, especially during monsoons. Yes, of course, I was coaching badminton a lot, but still, we had enough time to catch the latest movie. Street food was something we liked; *bhelpuri*, *kulfi*, and chilled sugarcane juice were welcome any time. We loved the spiking hot *dosas* and *samosas*, the *ragda pattice*, the simmering *jalebis* on a Sunday morning, and the omnipresent *vada pav*. There were social functions, and we had lots of invitations every month. The badminton tournament scene, of which I was a veteran, also invited us to witness the finals of many tournaments.

We went to see the theatre, and I also caught classical music shows, a passion with her. After all, she was an MA in Classical Music from Agra University. Moreover, she had a wonderful job teaching music at the prestigious Bhartiya Vidya Bhavan. She made the ultimate sacrifice of giving up the job, as she wanted to look after me full-time. I cannot thank her enough. There was nothing much to do for me except for writing; how much can you do it? What got me was the ennui, sheer boredom. I just did not know how to spend time. Staring at walls throughout the day does you no good. Afterall, how much Deepti and I could talk about?

Yes, I must mention how close relatives and friends behave once you are wheelchair user. They visit you initially, show great concern, and visit you for a few months or more. This concern is genuine, and some friends/relatives come a few times bringing gifts and flowers. But then, how long can they continue coming to see you? Slowly but surely, they stop visiting you. Some relatives or friends you consider close to you don't come. It happened to me, too. Ultimately, you are left alone to fight the demons parked inside your brain, rearing their ugly faces now and then to torment and torture you.

As an Urdu poet wrote once,

"Maine zindagi ko itna to pehchana hai,
Dard me akele hain, Khushi mein zamana hai

(I have recognised life so much,
I am alone in pain; there is a world in happiness)."

How true is it!

TWELVE

One day Satya and Rajaram came to meet me. They looked agitated and, with no pleasantries exchanged, immediately got down to business. "Sir ji, you know the case of Fazil Ahmed and Ahmed Hussain? They are friends from the fifth standard as they studied in the same special school. They both are polio survivors and walk with the use of callipers. They have joined the government-run Asher Global College for higher studies at Juhu, Gulmohar Road, where the principal is Molly Khatwani. Her deputies are Ganpati Rao and Rajeswar Shah. Rao is looking after public relations and marketing classes. At the same time, Rajeswar Shah heads the public administration classes and takes care of college administration and maintenance.

The college recently installed a lift in the four-story-high building. The lift, however, is to be used only by the 60-odd teaching staff. A notice to that effect had been put up on each floor. Fazil and Ahmed are taking public administration classes as they want to join IAS after graduation. The boys approached the principal to allow them to use the lift as they found it difficult to climb the three stories to reach their class on time.

Khatwani forwarded the note to her legal advisor Ramu Bhai

Merchant, and copy to Rajeswar Shah. These two and Ganpati Rao, a special invitee to the meeting, have advised against allowing the boys to use the lift. Why set up precedence, they argued. Tomorrow some other students may want to use the lift with any other excuse.

You have a name, a strong background, and a well-known personality. We want you to come and talk to the principal to sort this out," Satya Prakash said. There was real sincerity in his voice. I would have said 'yes' in any case because this would give me some respite from the utter boredom that had enveloped me for some time now. I looked forward to meeting the principal, Khatwani, and her team. We sought an appointment with her and reached the college at the correct time.

The fathers of Fazil and Ahmed were also with us; they had met us at the college entrance. So, we waited at the reception, three wheelchair users and the two fathers. Khatwani made us wait for an hour and did not even bother apologising for making us sit outside for an hour and not offering water or tea, which is common decency. That showed the woman's character as obnoxious.

We had decided beforehand that I would be the official spokesperson of the team and that only I would speak. Anyhow, she was alarmed to see so many of us. The wheelchairs did not fit in, and she opened the conference room and called for her troops to join us. Led by the old man, Merchant, Shah, and Rao marched in. Her secretary Sangeeta was called to take notes of the proceedings.

Looking at the two fathers, she said, "You have brought Mr Satya Prakash and Mr Rajaram again. Please introduce these gentlemen to us before we start this meeting." I was introduced, and my background was given correctly. "So, Mr. Sharma, what is your interest in this meeting? We had made our stand clear last time." "Madam," I said, "I am the spokesperson for the two boys and their father. I have been told about the meeting you had with these two fathers; however, I feel their concern was not addressed properly. With all due respect to the college and you, Madam, I think your decision is not based on real humanity; boys cannot reach their class on time in the current situation."

Khatwani looked at Rao, the marketing and public relations man giving him a hint to come in. Clearing his throat, this tall, thin-looking man, in a very westernised drawl, reminded us of the last meeting, "I had explained last time that the management takes certain decisions that cannot be withdrawn. So, the decision stays, I am afraid." "I do not think that you are thinking of the serious repercussions you and the college will face if you go ahead with this decision, denying the boys to use the lift," I said. Media will have a field day, and your college will lose face. The world loves the Goliath and David story—Khatwani butted in between, saying they had taken permission from the State education board, and we were not wrong. Madam, you are not wrong on paper. I observed, however, you are morally wrong. These boys have to climb the stairs twice daily wearing their callipers. It will take them approximately 20-25 minutes to climb and enter the class. Your periods are for 50 minutes, which means they will have lost half the time. Next classes that follow also get affected."

Old man Merchant now sneaked in with a quick remark. "Don't worry about our classes. The decision has been made, and we will follow it. In any case, we can't change decisions just for two boys." I was really upset with this low cheap remark, "They are just not two boys, Sir. These boys are disabled, as the world knows. I would have desired more understanding from you. I am surprised at the fact that you are a lawyer. What sort of advice are you giving to her?"

Molly Khatwani, who had been restraining herself, now thought she had to say something. "Mr. Sharma, if you were in my position, you would understand. We have not taken any unilateral decision. I think we can wrap up now. In any case, there are no options left— I cut her off, "I am not in your position, Madam. Moreover, if I were, I would not have made this decision. But coming here, I think, why not bring their class to the ground floor? I saw many rooms when we came in inside the college premises." "They are all godowns," Shah interjected. "There is no space available in the college, said the administrator." The meeting was not going anywhere. Rajaram, who had not uttered a word till now and had a harrowing time as a student, observed wryly, "I think we should go because these people will never understand the trauma and problems of the people with disabilities. We are wasting our time here," and started to get up.

Satya Prakash also looked angry. "*Chalo* (let's go), Sir. We will go to the State Education Office tomorrow and complain about the behaviour of these people."

Khatwani, now simmering with anger, punched in and said, "You people do not understand the problems we will face if the two boys are allowed. It will set a bad precedent. How can we stop other students from using the lift? We will have no control." Rajaram, feeling good at our confrontation, said, "You people are weak. You try climbing three floors wearing callipers, and you will begin to understand our problems and how difficult it is for us to face perennial issues. Who are you to say we are weak?" Squeaked Khatwani in a shrill voice, getting angry. "How dare you?" She stared hard at Rajaram. "We will not have the two boys using the lift. The decision is made. If you all don't like this using lift problem, you are free to take admission elsewhere."

We were being dismissed. I felt sorry for Khatwani and her people for their myopic outlook on life. Their ignorance and lack of humanity, and I could not stop myself from remarking loudly, "Believe me, this is not the last you have seen or heard from me on this issue. You are pathetic, really lowlife scums who are inhuman."

THIRTEEN

It was time for action now. I suddenly felt elated. I had a purpose now, and working for the upliftment of people with disabilities would give me lots of satisfaction, I thought. Therefore, the first step in my mind was to analyse the situation as to why such people received the raw deal in terms of getting aid from both the state and central governments. Were they sufficiently represented in the various committees of the government? Why don't we see wheelchair users enjoying life here in India as they do abroad? Many questions reverberated in my mind. Realising that Satya and Rajaram were very active in the para-sports world, the best would be to talk to them.

The next afternoon we met. Moreover, frankly speaking, I did not know how much anger there was in the disabled community as they slowly learned about the plight of the two boys who were denied using the lift. Most in the community faced the same sort of problems sometimes. And many ideas were discussed with my two friends who had been in touch with some of the disabled community. We have to do something to bring it in front of the citizens. We had to hit their conscience. Let us talk to city-based journalists and get this story out through them.

I also felt that let us write a small 300 words item and place it at the Mumbai Journalists Association (MJA) office at Azad Maidan. Satya got this organised while Rajaram and I contacted journalists about the story. Very few journalists agreed to join our struggle; with World Cup cricket going on, their employers could not spare them. Satya could get to the MJA reception and leave a few copies to let them know what we were up to and how the local media could help us. The receptionist was taken aback when he read the note of Satya. "Is this happening in Mumbai in today's day and age?" he asked. Satya nodded in affirmative, and the excited receptionist said, "Don't worry, I will ensure this gets noticed." The MJA premises were empty right now, but by 8 pm, its bar would be filled as the hacks came in to quench their thirst after a hard day's work.

It had been decided that we would meet at the college entrance two days later. Rajaram had a brainwave. "There has to be a student council or a union in the college. Let them know what happened and what we planned to do." I agreed immediately, and he sent two of his 'non-disabled' swimming trainees with the task that they must deliver the note in the right hands; otherwise, we would lose the element of surprise.

Rajaram's students entered the college canteen and sat there sipping hot *chai*; they enquired from the canteen supervisor the names of the president and secretary of the students union and whether they would come to the canteen soon. "Yes," said the supervisor; when they come in, he will point out to the two boys. They waited patiently, listening to the chitchat few students just whiling away some time. Then what looked like a senior student walked in and was immediately shown major respect by the rest of the students. She took a corner table. Soon three more seniors strolled in and joined the first one. I looked at the supervisor with a questioning look, and he pointed out to the four, who were engrossed in an animated conversation. Our trainees introduced themselves and gave the note to the girl.

"My God. I cannot believe this. Is this happening in our college at this time and age? This is ridiculous." She was fuming, and she passed the note to the others. They all nodded assent and decided on a course of action. "We are with you. Tell us how we can support you guys." My phone number was passed to them. We discussed a few options on the phone, including a general strike and closing down the college. However, I wanted the principal to be humiliated for what she told us at our meeting. Therefore, after much discussion, we zeroed in on a game plan executed like a military exercise.

On the agreed day, just before the opening of the college gates, some 20 students from the student union formed a barricade in front of the main entrance at precisely 10 a.m., not allowing anyone to enter the premises. They carried placards that read 'SHAME ON YOU, MOLLY KHATWANI. YOU SHOULD RESIGN'. Soon, 10 polio-survivors suddenly appeared and joined the barricade led by Rajaram. This group had placards that said, 'WE ARE ALSO HUMAN. TREAT US WITH DIGNITY.'

Then I came with the two boys and their parents carrying a placard that read, 'KHATWANI MURDABAD, KHATWANI *HAI HAI* (DEATH TO KHATWANI).' I had a megaphone with me, and I addressed the crowd, telling them exactly what happened in my meeting with Khatwani. She normally came to the college at about 10.30 a.m. By then, about 70-80 people, curious passers-by, had stopped to listen to what was happening, and I kept repeating how this college and its principal, Molly Khatwani, had not allowed the two boys with disabilities to take the lift to their class on the third floor. The college is anti-divyang and inhuman. One interesting image I saw, which stayed in my mind for a long time, was a mini traffic jam outside the main gate as the protestors and some curious onlookers spread out onto the road. In some 5 minutes, we had a pile-up of almost 70 to 80 vehicles. Someone in the crowd asked me what do we want? There was nothing less than an apology from Khatwani. I bellowed in the megaphone and an immediate order to allow these two boys to use the lift.

At 10:30, the principal came and was gheraoed by the students and the Rajaram group, shouting "Khatwani *hai hai*." "I will never apologise. I have done nothing wrong. The state education board cleared this." The crowd, now restless, started to get angry at her stubborn attitude. "We will stay here for as long it takes and will not allow the college to function till you agree to apologise to the two boys," said the Student Union President.

Then something happened that we had not factored in. Permission from the local police station was not taken to gather in large numbers and hold public demonstrations. The police arrived and told us to stop our '*dharna* (protest),' and they got the main entrance opened. With a smirk on her face, Khatwani brushed past me, muttering, "You will not win. I will not resign or apologize." Therefore, we had to change strategy, but of one thing, I was sure that the public sympathy would be with us. All we had to do was to keep the momentum going. I was sure that some press and media reporters were present at the college entrance today, as I did see some video cameras. In any case, so many people were video shooting one could forward a clip to the news channels. It will not be long before a video goes viral.

We had a quick meeting and decided Satya would get us a police clearance for a peaceful demonstration at the same place. And we will now assemble in three different groups away from the entrance. And the student union will hold demonstrations inside the college, creating hungama.

A shot in the arm came as two news channels came out with a damning story holding Molly Khatwani responsible for this outrageous and inhumane treatment of the two boys. An enemy of people with disabilities screamed one channel. Another channel said the shocking behaviour of the principal; she must resign immediately. By 9 p.m., it was on national news. Tomorrow was going to be very interesting, I thought as I poured myself a stiff drink. The best thing that happened the next day was that the State Education Board distanced itself from the statement made by Khatwani that she had clearance from the authorities. Yes, said their spokesman, "We permitted the lift to be installed after seeing the structural fitness of the building. How they use the lift is their internal matter." So, Khatwani lied to us.

The next morning the Midday newspaper had the most scathing report. "This action of not allowing two boys with disabilities to use the lift was blatantly inhuman; this shows the sheer bigotry of the principal and her team. They must answer the nation about their myopic, narrow, anti-divyang outlook. Seeing this bias from an educational institution is shocking and bewildering."

What are we teaching our kids? The battle was over. Cornered from all sides, Khatwani had only two choices. Either resign and leave or apologize and retain her seat. She chose the latter but was very meek, docile, and chastened now; we had won a decisive victory and had a party. The power of the media was really strong and apparent. But what happened shortly nearly put us under state, if not national limelight.

FOURTEEN

My focus was now on improving the lot of people with disabilities. I saw my destiny entwined with theirs. I was beginning to understand the problems faced by them. There were so many types of such people. Each has its own set of problems, customised in a way. They were away from the national limelight as if hiding deliberately. They were shy and were afraid that people would make fun of them, and since they hardly interacted with the outside world, they became very vulnerable because they did not have any voice. At least, they feel so. How to make them mentally strong was an uphill task. However, it had to be done.

Now and then, incidents occur in the country, showing how callous and repulsive we can be in our behaviour towards people with disabilities. Who can forget the obnoxious way a 12-year-old boy was treated by Indigo Airlines recently? He was travelling from Ranchi to Hyderabad. Like any other cerebral palsy patient, the boy was drooling from the mouth. One airline staffer saw this and stopped the boy from putting his bag in the overhead bin. The boy and the parents were deplaned; this became a national scandal, and Indigo was fined five lakhs.

Then there was the case at Goa airport of a British wheelchair-using passenger hassled by two porters who wanted a 5,000 tip. They followed her and did not allow her to take her bags. No one rescued her, and she had to pay the amount. Reading all this in the news, the community and the brothers and sisters with disabilities tended to withdraw further into their shells.

The Arunima Sinha story was one such, which shook the very foundation of the people with disabilities. Arunima, a national volleyball player going to play a tournament by train, tried to foil a robbery and, in retaliation, was thrown out off the train in April 2011 by the robbers. The doctors tried hard to ensure that she did not lose any limb and had no option but to amputate one leg below the knee. As she recovered, she tried to analyse her future. Very fond of sports, she knew she couldn't pursue any active sports now. A friend told her about a mountain-climbing club where she could learn to climb mountains despite her condition.

Desperate to do something, she used a wheelchair to the club and met the senior trainers and coaches. Run by the army, this mountaineering club was very professional in its approach to climbing. They assured her that her disability would not come in the way. Her zeal, enthusiasm, and natural sporting instinct helped her to learn the ropes quickly.

She took up the challenge of climbing Mt. Everest to the astonishment of all people, and she became a living legend as she became the first female amputee in the world to climb Everest. Yet, this very legend was humiliated and mocked for her disability when she went to have *darshan* (sight) of the lord at the well-known shrine at Mahakal temple in Ujjain, Madhya Pradesh. She wanted to visit one of the *jyotirlingas* of Shiva which are spread across the country, and which are visited by devotees and travellers around the world.

In a report by NDTV on 27/12/2017, she said that she felt

humiliated and she cried profusely because she was not allowed to enter the sanctum sanctorum. The security guards did not allow her to enter as per the administration's instructions. She was wearing a track bottom, to which the authorities had an objection. "I told them I had lost a leg and would take only a minute for my darshan. But they insisted that I was improperly dressed and almost threw me out. I have never felt so humiliated before in my life. This pain was much more intense than my pain during the climb."

*****

There have been many stories about disabled being denied jobs in the private sector. They are found wanting, and compared to the normal worker, their output is much less. And, of course, the shabby treatment given to many disabled by National Airlines must be mentioned. The Director General of Civil Aviation (DGCA) has recently passed a rule that no airline can stop passengers with any disability or lack of mobility from boarding a flight. So, there is a great focus now on airlines, and they cannot do much *hera-pheri* (foul play).

So, what and where can we make an impact? That was the idea. So, we met often and, over drinks, thought out loud, coming up with some interesting solutions.

One day, while we debated India's performance at the ICC T20 in Australia, breaking news appeared on the screen about a Muslim reservation bill that could be passed, ensuring a ten per cent reservation in government jobs. Reservations—reservations, reservations that were all nowadays. Every segment of society wants a piece of the shrinking pie. The funny thing was that some upper castes wanted to be listed backwards just to get into a reservation. Life could be so ironic. These same upper castes would decimate the lower ones without remorse in the villages. I listened to this news on reservation, and the seed of an idea started germinating.

I asked Satya how many disabled lived in the country and their percentage in the population. We represented every caste and creed, or dharma, in our community. We were not Hindu or Muslim, Sikh or Christian people with disabilities, and so on. We were just people. *Bas.* That is it. So how many were we?

Satya did his research and came back in a few days. "The total percentage of people with disabilities in India is roughly 7%, not counting the mentally challenged as they fall in different categories', he reported. However, we count the golden senior citizens, aged 75 and above, who require as much attention as any disabled. We will be roughly 15 % of the population. The golden senior citizen has mobility problems, hearing, and visual problems apart from so many others.

"Well, that was a sizeable chunk of Indians. 15% of 1.4 billion meant 210 million strong if I am correct. That is a sizeable number, whichever way you look at it. It easily is more than the total population of most countries. I chewed at this figure for some time. Why do we not matter to the government or the authorities? If we are so numerous? The Muslims were less than we were or perhaps almost equal in population but politically strong. The Dalits were another group who were strong and who mattered.

So many small groups mattered, as politically, they knew how to milk the cow. But actually, what is the mantra that makes them relevant? In one word, 'UNITY'. Unity in front of any other group, Unity for fighting the system, and Unity in doing whatever work the leader of their group gave them. One factor common to all the religious groups was that they all had a political party. If the Muslim League represented the Muslims, the Bahujan Samaj party was the party of the Dalits, and the Shiromani Akali Dal stood for the Sikhs. However, we had nothing. So, if the government wanted to talk to us, whom do they talk to? This was the dilemma we had to address, and that too immediately. By now, I was accepted as the ad hoc leader of our group.

I told my group what was on my mind and asked them to come the next day for a meeting. Apart from Satya and Rajaram, we now had Ravin Panjwani, principal of a blind school, Amrita, who was in charge of the government-sponsored *Anathalya* (orphanage) where children who had lost their parents were allowed to stay. As well as Abdul Hamid, an ex-army man, in charge of the hostel for delinquents, basically for children under 18 years of age who had committed a crime and could not be tried as they were considered minors in the eyes of the law.

Rajaram had retired from Western Railway, but his scientific bent of mind and keen business acumen were well used as he converted vehicles to hand control. It was a good business as many disabled could drive cars if they had clearance from the regional transport office. He converted 40/50 vehicles each year, bringing him a handsome amount of money. Satya Prakash had a *kirana* (grocery) shop given to him by the BEST Company of the state government. It was given to him by the BEST management to secure his future and in appreciation for the 40 years of hard work his father had put into the BEST company as a bus driver.

FIFTEEN

"Friends, I have been thinking for the last two or three weeks about how to get noticed in the country and get more benefits for our community. And I have concluded that we must have a political party representing us to the world. You take any minority community like Muslims, Dalits, Sikhs, etc., and they get all the goodies from the government because they fight for it. They have the Muslim League, Bahujan Samaj Party, Shiromani Akali Dal, and so on.

I think we should also go for one. The party will unite people with disabilities under one banner and give them an identity. We will speak as one, under one leadership. What do you all think about it?" They all took some time to digest what I had said. Then suddenly, the room was buzzing with excited voices. Everyone was talking at the same time. The consensus was that this idea was brilliant and should be implemented immediately.

Ever the cautious man, Rajaram observed that we must have a party name. Satya said, "We must do some market research and find out from the people with disabilities what they think. He said he would take a week and bring the results of his research. Amrita wanted to think about this before coming back with an answer, but she added that the idea is good, but will it be workable?

Abdul Hamid, typically aggressive as a soldier, was all for it and said, “Let’s start immediately. Why wait? This is what we had been waiting for. Once people with disabilities know there are some serious people behind this, they will all support it.”

Ravin had a passion for maths, was a tax expert, and was ever the finance man who thought aloud, “This is all very good, but how will we finance this movement?” But the meeting was good, I felt. We agreed to meet after a week, and everyone was supposed to have name options for the party by then. The days went by fast, with everyone busy doing their homework for the meeting.

Forming a national party and getting it registered takes a long time. At the national level, the party has to win a certain percentage of votes before you put in papers for registration. It is easier at the state level, or the best for a new party is to fight Vidhan Sabha elections or a bye poll which can happen if a sitting MLA expires or resigns. But in any case, a beginning had to be made.

In our meeting, we got to hear the viewpoints of all five of us. Satya went first. “Every disabled person I met agreed that we must have a party to represent them. They all wanted to join the party. The idea appeals to them. I met over 500 potential volunteers. So, I would say that let’s do it. We will be successful 100%.”

Rajaram came out with two names; both were good, the National Divyang Party and the Vikas Party for People with Disabilities. Abdul Hamid simply said that he agreed with Satya. “Let’s start work on this asap.” Amrita, who is normally very quiet, “I believe we can start launching the party now.” Still, people associated with it must be clean and above reproach. Ravin said, “We need to collect at least Rs 50 lakh.” He had an idea of how we could go about it.

Since this party will help all the people with disabilities, let them fund by donating Rs 500 each directly to our bank account, which we can open anytime. It was a brilliant thought and appreciated by each one of us. Very many people with disabilities in Mumbai and surrounding areas already knew about our victory against Molly Khatwani and the two boys who were permitted to use the lift. I was sure that funding from the man on the street would come.

I was the host; therefore, I was last to go. I, too, had done some homework. I told them a state bye poll for Vidhan Sabha would be held within 6 months. If we are serious about launching a political party for people with disabilities, let us try to enter a candidate in this by-poll. Let us see how we will get there. And yes, I had a name for the party, Divyang Unnati Sangthan or DUS. Loosely translated, it meant 'party for the progress and prosperity of the people with disabilities.' Everyone was happy with the name. It meant—a party for progress and prosperity for divyang. So now, we had a name and a focus. The next six months are going to be interesting.

SIXTEEN

Before anything, we had to gear for another skirmish with authority, and we did not have to wait long. Two young visually impaired girls were late in coming out of the Braille classes they were attending. Neighbours in Azad Nagar slums at Versova, near Juhu beach. It was wintertime in Mumbai, and nights came in early. In their eagerness to reach the safety of their home as early as possible, they missed one turn and then got confused.

The National Association for The Blind had a unique thing called the distress signal, similar to a pepper spray can that is used by many women, who could unleash the spray on the face of the assaulter, making him momentarily blind. For visually impaired persons, the device developed was called The Distress Signal. Just as big as a mobile phone, it emits a high-decibel shriek, which indicates a visually impaired person is in trouble and seeking help.

In a way, it was like the SOS signal sent by aeroplanes, ships, and long-distance trucks that were in trouble. The ones used by women could scream in the language of her choice of few words to draw attention. In Hindi, the screams were *"Mujhe koi bachao! Koi bachao.* (Someone saves me! Please save me)." The voice could carry up to 30 metres, enough to get help. However, these devices were expensive, costing Rs 1,200 each, which included the customs duty of Rs 500. The National Association of Blind wanted these duties removed immediately for visually impaired women and had moved the State Government, which had the power to take that action. However, it was like falling on deaf ears. Sadly, many letters from the association had gone unanswered by State and Central Governments.

Two years had gone by, and many instances had taken place that should have shamed the police, the government, or any other agencies. Still, no one was bothered since the survivors came from the poor section of society, like two girls walking as fast as their legs could carry them. Nevertheless, they were lost as they had taken the wrong turn and entered a neighbouring slum called Vijay Nagar. The canes used by them normally worked from memory. On their usual route, the cane knew every bump, every crevice, and every speed breaker, but this cane was as lost as the girls on a new route.

A big SUV painted white was parked at a road junction up ahead. Ramesh Chadha, younger brother of MLA Suresh Chadha, sat with his friends Sanjeev and Rajeev, drinking beer. The boys were slightly drunk, laughing away at old jokes. Suddenly, Ramesh saw two girls walking slowly and tentatively, unsure of themselves. The girls were young and well-built; he also saw they had these walking canes tapping ahead of them, normally used by people who are visually impaired. A brief but clear signal passed between those three. Leaving the SUV's door open, Sanjeev and Rajeev quickly went to walk behind the girl while Ramesh went in front of them and asked if the two were lost.

"Yes," one said. "We wanted to go to Azad Nagar, Bengali Chawl," but they had taken a wrong turn and were now lost. "Don't worry; we are also from there and can give you a lift." At a signal from Ramesh, Rajeev and Sanjeev caught hold of the waist of the girl in front and pushed them into the car in a matter of few seconds. The girls screamed and shouted as they were being molested. "Let's go to our usual haunt at the top of the hill." Instructed Ramesh from the back seat as he tried to snatch the upper cloth of one of the girls. Rajeev, who was driving, looked into the rear-view mirror, and grinned as his eyes met those of Ramesh, full of lust. Not knowing where they were being taken, the girls cried and kept shouting to be taken to Azad Nagar. "All in good time." Said Rajeev. As this was watched by Hemu, a waiter at the beer and wine retail outlet just ahead, had watched them as he came out to relieve himself. There had been only a few buyers till now as it was just 7 pm, and the patrons started coming in to buy only after 9 p.m.; the management does not like any of the sales counters boys to be absent from the counter during the peak timings between 8-10 p.m.

Hemu raised the alarm and rushed to the proprietor, narrating what he had just seen and asked the owner to contact the number 100 and report to the police immediately. The law enforcement officer who came on-line was a calm professional. In turn, he got hold of the constable on duty at the notorious Vijay Nagar chowki, where four beat constables were on duty near the exit. They saw the SUV approaching them and motioned the driver to stop. However, Rajeev pressed hard on the accelerator, trying to scare the policeman, who jumped out of the way. Rajeev, however, did not see a truck slowly reversing out from a garage to go towards the main road. By the time he realised that he was going too fast on this narrow street, the SUV hit a parked car that had come in the way of the SUV and moved towards the main gate. As the vehicle came out of Azad Nagar, a police vehicle from the local police station started chasing it. It caught the SUV when it hit a parked truck under darkness due to the streetlight not working.

The policemen were stunned to see two visually impaired girls in the back seat with crumpled clothes not in the correct order. They screamed and said they were visually impaired and had been kidnapped and molested in the car. The constables tied the boys to the SUV and waited for a senior inspector to arrive. Now slowly returning to his senses, Ramesh realised this was a dicey situation. He beckoned one of the constables and identified himself as the younger brother of MLA Suresh Chadha. "Don't file a case; I will get you tons of cash."

However, the constables told him that Sr Inspector Chetan Gaekwad would arrive any moment, and he was above reproach. They advised that he follows the law vigorously, so don't even try to offer him cash. Inspector Gaekwad knew of Ramesh and ignored him when he came to the site. A case was to be filed, but since a police detainee could make a phone call, Gaekwad knew what would happen soon. He had called for the girls' parents to come to his office and explain what he wanted from them.

It was his insurance against what was going to happen soon. True enough, a car screeched to a halt at the police station, and DCP Chauhan came bouncing in and indicated to Gaekwad to follow him to his cabin.

"So, what is the scene? What happened?" The DCP started, "Sir, the three boys had kidnapped the two visually impaired girls and molested them. They were quite drunk. I have asked for tests to be done on them. Luckily, they could not go to a secluded place and commit rape. A police van chased them, and they hit a truck in haste. "One of the boys—" Before he could finish, the Chauhan's phone rang.

He was very submissive as he talked, saying, "Yes, Sir. Yes, Sir." a few times. To a question, he replied, "Inspector Gaekwad has the case—Yes, Sir. I will." "That was the Commissioner. He says that we should not have an FIR on this. FIR is the abbreviated form of the First Information Report. Detain them for some time and then release them. Understood?"

As if on cue, they heard some commotion outside, slogans being raised against the police. It was the parents of the two girls, accompanied by 30/35 persons in their neighbourhood, demanding justice. Gaekwad thought the timing could not be better.

The DCP was in a fix. The survivors had come to file the FIR, as they wanted the perpetrators to be punished as per law. Rape is a very heinous crime. Ramesh Chadha, with Rajeev and Sanjeev, was looking for at least 14 years behind bars. And the survivors were helpless visually impaired girls who could not defend themselves even if they wanted.

The media is going to have a field day tomorrow. It was already past 10 at night. Most papers would have been printed by this time, but there was no such deadline for TV networks. They got the girls to talk about their turmoil and the nightmare they had faced. Meanwhile, at the police station, the girls' fathers and some supporters stayed put until the FIR was registered.

What was to be done, Gaekwad enquired from his boss DCP Chauhan, who was almost constantly on the phone. Suresh Chadha, The MLA, was from the ruling party and wanted his brother out of the police station immediately. He was on his tenth phone call to the Commissioner and was not mincing words. "Are you listening to me or not? *Tere ko aisi jagah transfer kara doonga jahan par rone ke alava kuch nahi milta hai. Yahan par lakhon kamata hai har mahine. Jara soch le.*" (I will transfer you to such a place where you will only get to cry. Here, you get to earn lakhs per month. Give it a thought.)

He threatened the Commissioner, who in turn put pressure on

the DCP. At 3 am, Suresh Chadha entered the station and demanded to meet Ramesh. *"Bhaiya, mujhse badi galti ho gayi hai. Mujhe maaf kar do* (I have made a huge mistake. Please forgive me.)", sobbed Ramesh, who received a resounding slap from his brother. "You very well know that the cabinet reshuffle will take place soon. And I am slated to come in as a (MOS) with an independent charge or as a MOS in a big ministry. And you go on molesting girls without thinking what good it will do to my career." One more slap landed on the cheek of Ramesh.

DCP and Gaekwad were silent witnesses to this family drama. Suresh understood well enough that FIR has to be filed, but the police can write in such a way that any case cannot be made. And ordered the DCP to do so.

SEVENTEEN

This is where we came in. The TV news channels were blasting away at the system, the pure negligence by the police. The stories were even more emotional since the two girls were visually impaired. With the media braying for the blood of Ramesh and his cronies, it was easy to guess what the morning would bring. Yes, hundreds of people had landed at the police station. We had discussed on the phone what was to be done. And how we could help the cause of the girls.

Ravin came up with a good idea of bringing his school girls who were visually impaired. He will protest with one simple placard saying, 'DUS demands the harshest punishment for the criminals. Is our future safe?'. Ravin also sat with his school girls in case some journalist or TV wanted to do a story. His handmade placard read,' DUS got justice for the two boys who were physically challenged at Ashar College at Juhu. We will get it here also.'

Satya and Rajaram, as one pair, and Amrita and Abdul, as the other pair, had taken upon themselves the task of handing out copies of the note they had written highlighting the DUS and distributing it to all sundry at the police station protest. We had to derive as much benefit as possible to fight the bye poll. I had another task to do. I had numerous copies of notes that I had written, saying the state and central government were equally guilty as the three boys.

Why the Distress Signal Can should be so expensive? Why is the import duty so high that these girls cannot afford it? They would not be in such a situation. If they had the Can, someone would have surely come to the rescue and protected them. So, the Commerce Minister of Central and State governments was equally guilty.

The National Association of Blinds had tried for years to get a waiver of duty for visually impaired girls but to no avail. The authorities, to be, were simply not interested. So, the battle was on. Most of Mumbai would know what DUS stood for by tomorrow. In my note, I asked immediate resignation of the State Commerce Minister Deepak Kamble, as he was guiltier of the two.

In the night, MLA Suresh thought he would unlock the back door and simply walk away with Ramesh from the police station. But inspector Gaekwad had anticipated this and had the back door locked up. At the crack of dawn, Suresh knew that the game was over and the FIR would be filed. There was no escape.

In the morning, the bomb exploded as channel after channel carried various reports on the dastardly act. Ravin has become quite the hero as he articulated our motto of helping the divyangs. Our party was formed to give confidence to all physically challenged. All media present, had received the information about us and were quite intrigued by the formation of DUS.

When the newspapers came out, the crime had caught the main headlines. There were reports and interviews of various people, including Women's Welfare Associations, Women Against Rape, Women United For Domestic Dignity, etc. Police spokesman announced that they would ask for the strongest penalty and punishment for the three culprits. The fact that the helpless girls were visually impaired evoked deep anger in Mumbai.

My stand on the Distress signal theory was also striking home. People were angry about this system, where no one could be blamed for wrong decisions. I also talked about the "observer tours" where crores of taxpayers' rupees were wasted. The money saved from these jamborees could be spent on women's safety. I said these observation tours should be banned, and all and sundry echoed the same sentiments.

I was also hitting home when I was asked for the resignation of Deepak Kamble since he refused to cut down import duty and make it cheaper for visually impaired girls all over India to protect themselves.

*****

The case went to court in the usual way. The boys were given bail after 3 months; it was an open-and-shut case anyway. I was sure that when the trial started and judgement came, they would be sentenced to at least 14 years in jail. But the trial will be at least after a year. There were huge backlogs of cases in the courts in India.

Meanwhile, our party's name was becoming well-known in the community.

And my demand for Deepak Kamble's resignation was gaining more traction. Demands for his resignation were getting shrill and had started hitting where it hurt. His carefully crafted image was getting battered. One day as I had anticipated, I got a call from him. He wanted to meet me. I told him that my full group would come with me. He agreed but very reluctantly.

When we reached his office, and after exchanging pleasantries, he came abruptly to the point. "What have you got against me? You have been belittling and degrading me in the media for many days." He looked at me, a flash of anger passing though his eyes. He was a powerful Cabinet Minister, not to be taken lightly.

"It is nothing personal. It is just that you have not reduced the price of the Distress Signal Can, and the steep price is not affordable for many poor visually impaired girls. They require relief and help—" He cut me short. "It is not easy to reduce duty. And we are not the only ones; the centre also is involved in this. But you people are making me look like the chief culprit and anti-blind, which I am not." Amrita interjected, "But you are anti-blind and anti-divyang. You could have decided on your own, but you did not do so. In fact, and you will probably know this, the central government had withdrawn the central duty and given an exemption to people with disabilities who could drive and wanted to buy a car. The first exemption was given to the famous female para-athlete Malthi Holla. The exemption was for Rs 1,60,000.

For your lack of action, God knows how many poor girls must have been molested or even raped." What are you saying, madam? Is it because of me the girls are in danger?" The minister was getting a bit agitated. "Yes, you are culpable for bringing danger to the girls. And you run your department most inefficiently. For four months, you did not reply to the National Association of Blind. If you had answered the letters, a solution could have been found."

Ravin is now enjoying the site of the minister squirming in his chair. "There will be a loss of revenue to the state. I have to ensure that the state has enough money rolling in at hand and the various welfare schemes that we run are not lacking in finance."

It was the turn for Satya to chip in with his style. "I do not understand, Minister. You are saying you have enough money to run the welfare schemes, yet you do not want to give welfare to the visually impaired girls." I thoroughly enjoyed this verbal banter between my team and the minister, who was rattled by the attack on him and his thinking. But the best was yet to come. When the meeting was getting heated up, Amrita served a googly. Before that, I pitched in and said, "Minister, I think if you resign and take responsibility for your inaction, so to say, you will save a lot of grief to yourselves and your party. You may even come back stronger after your next Vidhan Sabha elections."

Really worked up, Damle swallowed a bit and sounded bitter, "You think this is a game of children to win elections and become a cabinet minister? Why should I resign or cut the cost of the Can for distress signal? It is selling well and bringing good revenue." Amrita Speaking, I feel you should distribute the Can free of cost. The safety and dignity of our girls are more important than earning money," was the googly bowled by Amrita.

The minister was choking, almost sputtering now, unable to understand the pincer attack of the DUS. " No, no, this cannot be done. How can we offer it free of cost? There are millions of women in the state. All women between 15 to 50 would like to carry the Distress Signal Can with them—we will go bankrupt", Hamid, the soldier, butted in to make a statement before his staff ushered us out." India is not a poor country that cannot look after its citizens. For the safety of the women who were divyang and the rest of the females, the DUS will start a vigorous campaign.

An angry Damle stood up and yelled, "You divyang will not succeed in this blackmail, blatant blackmail. You have no power." I said. It was my turn to speak. "You have not seen the power of a divyang. Just wait until we divyangs, or people with disabilities, unite under the banner of DUS. Then the power of the divyang will be unleashed." I had the last word as Damle glared at me.

EIGHTEEN

I called a press conference the very next day to tell the media that a very important message had to be sent out by DUS. There was a good representation of the media in the press conference. Simply because of the two instances in which we had taken the side of the underdog and got justice for them. The case of the two boys who were not allowed to use the college lift even though they were polio survivors and walked with callipers.

And the case of the visually impaired girls who were molested by a drunken trio, one of whom was the brother of the sitting MLA. But with our party DUS entering the ring to help the survivors, the whole scene changed in favour of the survivors. And yes, okay, the name of DUS was being touted everywhere. We were finding acceptance in the world of people with disabilities. That was our aim to start with. If anything, we had not programmed for such an early acceptance among our community.

The Rs 500 donation for membership had started pouring in. We already had some 4,500 members, who also agreed to be volunteers when required. The media knew there would be some interesting announcements from the DUS. Therefore, by 6 in the evening, the venue was packed. I walked in with my team, welcomed the media, and started by highlighting our journey so far.

DUS was born to give voice to the divyang. I accepted that before I became a wheelchair user, I had never talked about the problems faced by the physically challenged people. That is true, even though I had authored a book called 'Courage Beyond Compare' which highlighted the laurels brought to India by para-athletes. Still, I had also written about problems faced by people with disabilities. It was only after I was declared physically challenged, did I see what is the meaning of ramps. Since I did not need it before, I did not see whether ramps existed. Now I know how important these ramps are.

Then the lifts in the buildings. People take these simple things for granted, but these are life savers for you. Then let's talk of public transport, which was pathetic, to say the least, even today. We can't go anywhere as we can't enter buses or trains. What is the government doing? They can't provide even these basic things to us. You take the roads now. The non-disabled have to hop, step, and jump on the potholes. If you all find walking on our city roads difficult, imagine what a nightmare it must be for the divyang.

The government spends hundreds of crores on these observation jamborees where the ministers and MLAs of the ruling party go abroad to observe why Europe or the USA is better than us. They do not see how is the disabled treated over here; this has been on for many decades.

Then you all must have seen the mobile entourage which travels with the Chief Minister. At least 15 vehicles and 40-50 police guards and NSG commandos travel with the CM when on tour. The PM has a cavalcade of 25/35 vehicles and scores of NSG commandos. Why do they require so much security when they are *netas* (ministers) of the people? Hundreds of crores of taxpayers' money are wasted like this. And yet, they always cry that they do not have any money to make our lives easier.

Then you have these huge hoardings welcoming the party head or other dignitaries of the ruling party. These politicians just want to show how diligently they work for you; full-page advertisements in leading newspapers.

Arrey, this is their job. Why is it necessary to highlight it? You are expected to do your work. The voters are not stupid. They know who is working and who isn't. From 1947, when we got *azadi* (freedom) from the British, we have seen many governments come and go. Different political parties were craving for and getting power from the people. But there has been no change in the status of divyangs with disabilities. The rest of the Indians have prospered but not us. The roads are the same, public transport is pathetic, lack of ramps, no lifts in most buildings, lack of employment, and so on. The problem, as I understand, is that people with disabilities are terrified as physically they cannot fight. Because of this major problem, they hardly mingle with the outside world, living and reliving their miseries in isolation.

Take my example. I was a terror on the badminton courts in India and even abroad; fit, fast, and strong. But what can I do today if attacked by a person? Nothing, zilch.

So the divyangs were never a vote bank. The DUS was formed basically for this purpose only. To give us a sense of unity in voting and try to get power politically, which can be used for the good of my community. The DUS will be the voice of people with disabilities. I am happy to tell you that we are already 4,500 members strong.

So, coming now to the purpose of calling you all today is to announce in gigantic proportions. We had a meeting with the Minister of Commerce, Deepak Damle. We have been asking him to cut the duty on the Distress Signals and resign because of the Can of Distress Signal controversy. It was not a happy meeting in his office on his invitation. He refused to cut the duty or resign and was rude to us. On one issue, he got very that angry. This was the proposal my colleague Amrita gave to protect the women of this country, irrespective of their colour, caste, or creed. And since she proposed, it is only correct that she announces it.

A surprised Amrita looked at me as I invited her to the microphone. With a smile, she took my place. "I will not take much of your time, my friends, as I have little to say. I have strongly suggested to the hon'ble minister that the Distress Signals Can be provided free of cost to the women of our country. It does not matter how much the cost is to India. We are a big, proud, and rich country and can easily provide the protection required for our women; this is all I have to say."

The silence was broken by the buzz of excitement that slowly engulfed the venue. Everyone from the media had a question to ask. While the females in the media made a beeline to Amrita, others leapt to *gherao* (encircle) me. But we had decided not to give any interviews but to occasionally release news from our side so that interest in DUS remained unabated. So with our smiles intact, we bid goodbye to the media and moved out.

As expected, the PC was big news in the newspapers the next day. And TV channels were breaking news within the hour. At least, in the State, we were now a name to be taken seriously. We looked good to be a strong player in the bye poll about a month away now, and Amrita was the heroine as far as the media was concerned. The DUS and Amrita had put the government on notice; They had to say yes otherwise risk half the votes in the country going away from them. We felt good.

NINETEEN

The rule for the bye poll is that the seat cannot be vacant for more than six months. The people must have representation both in the Vidhan Sabha and the Lok Sabha. The constituency which had fallen vacant after the sudden death of the sitting MLA Raj Kishore was the Vidhan Sabha constituency of Northwest Mumbai. And as per the tradition of many political parties, the spouse was offered the ticket to fight on behalf of the party. The idea was that the emotional vote goes to the spouse. One reason why Indian society was socially lacking behind was that these elections were still fought on caste, gender, emotions, and religious basis, and not based on merit or qualifications.

So, for all and sundry, Nandini Kishore was as good as home. But we were not entering the fray to lose out. We intended to give our best possible shot. In favour of DUS were two main factors. At last count, there were some 1,24,000 people with disabilities, potential voters and another 98,000 registered voters of age 75 and above. There are a potential 2,22,000 voters in our kitty, and out of the 18,76,500 registered voters in this constituency, 48.3% were women.

I was quite happy with this breakdown. The second factor was that by now, we had 12,375 registered members in the DUS, and all had vowed to do volunteer work in the constituency if required.

Many of these members were non-disabled, yet they understood the importance of giving the divyang the best possible help so that they may stand on their feet and contribute to society. These members/volunteers knew the importance of this bye-election for DUS. We have to put up a good show. With Mumbai almost always in the national limelight, a good showing here will give us pan-India publicity, just like the AAP Party in New Delhi. The announcement of the election date could come any time. So, the time had come to select our candidate.

A meeting had been called for the same purpose, to debate the best possible candidate. We were the first officials of the party. We left it to Satya, Amrita, and Hamid to make the right choice. At the same time, Rajaram, Ravin, and I toured the length and breadth of the constituency, talking to the voters and trying to find their mood. Feedback was generally favourable to us.

DUS was well known; at least the women had come to know, especially about our fight for the two visually impaired girls. And Amrita's statement about the Can of Distress Signal to be given free to all women had reverberated well with women of all hues. So, with Nandini Kishore already selected as the ruling party candidate, we also needed to select ours. It was apparent that our candidate for the bye-election must be dramatic and had hardly been seen fighting an election before. But who was well known without a doubt in the divyang community? It would not be amiss to say that he or she was even revered in some sections.

*****

We all met after a week to select the candidate. The meeting went on for hours without concluding. After a break of an hour for lunch, we started pounding our heads again. What was decided was that the candidate had to be a divyang, well-known in the community, and one who could make politics his or her career was a tall order, but we wanted the best possible person.

By night, Rajaram came up with the best possible candidate with most of our sought virtues. His name was Sitara Chand Gopal, in short, he was called Tara. and he was born totally deaf and visually impaired. He had vision in one eye only, and that too 50% in. He was an honouree of the International Marathon Swimming Hall of Fame. He won the crown of Open Water Swimming, completing the English Channel, the Sri Lanka Channel, and the New York Marathon Swim.

Awarded by the government, a national award in 1990, he was a real hero of not just the divyang community but the entire nation. We met him at his office and explained what we wanted. He immediately agreed and accepted the challenge of fighting the election for the DUS. With this part over and feeling pleased with our effort, we then started working on the other aspects of the looming election. Our focus now was getting our message across to the electorate. Prime importance was that they should know what DUS stood for and why it was important to vote for us.

Sitara Chand was in his element as he vowed the crowds, speaking to them through an interpreter. The crowd just loved Sitara, as the number of selfies he had to pose for after his speech was over was an indication. After all, he was a national icon, and he was a top-level sportsman; who had unlimited stamina. He did almost 10-12 rallies nonstop daily, way more than Nandini Kishore, the main rival, could do.

The much-awaited bye-election date was announced; there were just 20 days to go.

Our campaign moved into top gear, with volunteers spreading throughout the breadth and length of the constituency.

We devised a questionnaire with 6 simple questions the probable voter needed to read and understand before answering.

Q1. Do you know what DUS stands for?

Q2. Which party stands for equal rights for men and women?

Q3. Which contestant is pie honest and a national divyang swimming icon fighting the election for the DUS?

Q4. Are you happy with the way this government works?

Q5. Will you vote for this government? Do you feel that time for change has come?

Q6. (Only for women) Being a woman, do you think the stand of DUS was correct in the sensational case of the two visually impaired girls? Should the Distress Signals Can be distributed free of cost?

With 12,000 election volunteers at work, led by the bubbly Sitara, we touched almost 6 lakh voters. We did not have money to run full-page ads in the newspapers or purchase TV slots like the ruling party was doing. But we were not deterred because, in any case, I felt that face-to-face contact with the voters was personal and better.

TWENTY

Sitara Chand wanted a TV debate against Nandini Kishore and said so to a few media reporters. The media flashed this news, and the people of the constituency eagerly waited for Nandini to accept the challenge. So, as we waited for her decision, the routine electioneering continued vigorously. Of course, Nandini had no option but to accept the debate challenge. People would have thought she was afraid and running away like a coward if she had said no. As we were debating, something happened that our attention was diverted.

Now, Gulab Rao Patil is the Chief Administrative Head of the government-run Vidyalaya, and it's a hostel for mentally challenged orphans. He reported only to the Head Master. It was able to accommodate 150 girls of various ages and also had a place for 59 boys. These children had a very traumatic childhood. Many of them had been molested, tortured, and generally neglected. Some of the girls had been trafficked and rescued by the police. Most of these unfortunate children had no contact with anyone from their families.

Gulab Rao had known all this as he was in charge of running the Vidyalaya. He had details of each child and knew who had relatives, who would get visitors etc. The government had a good system laid down to help these kids. They had parole officers appointed by Magistrates whose job was to see that the child under their care became accepted by society as early as possible.

The scandal that hit the headlines nationwide, emanating from the Vidyalaya, was mind-boggling.

A court-appointed parole officer suspected something was wrong with the two girls under her charge. One of the girls complained of severe stomach ache. At the same time, the other one explained to the officer incoherently that she had missed her periods for two months. Alarmed at what she had heard, the officer immediately took permission from the Head Master of the institution to take the girls out for a medical check-up at the nearby government hospital. The doctor in charge of the emergency ward took the girls for examination. The test included the residual rectum test in determining if sodomizing had happened. They found the semen of two different persons in the pregnant girl.

Within 30 minutes, the test reports were with the parole officer. There it was in black and white, what she had suspected since hearing the complaint of these two. The girl who had missed her period was pregnant. The other one seemed to be having a vigorous sex life. It was now a police case. Both girls were minors and had little idea of what was happening. Both rape and sex with a minor are heinous crimes. The perpetrators here would go to jail for a long, long time.

Furthermore, both these minors were mentally challenged. The parole officer and the two girls were escorted to the police station, where female staff would question the girls, who, at seeing so many police personnel around them, became alarmed and upset and started crying; and they kept on shouting for 'chocolate uncle'.

Being mentally challenged, girls did not know what wrong they had done. The parole officer and the women constable tried to console them, but the crying did not stop. After hearing the story, the senior inspector in charge of the station, Vinayak Godambe, said they must go to the Vidyalaya and find out who this 'chocolate uncle' was.

Gulab Rao was on leave for two days and had gone to his village to do some purchases, especially a Ganpati *murti* (idol), for the Ganesh festival that was around the corner. He was a fervent Ganesh *Bhakt* (worshipper) who believed the Elephant God was kind to him. He had decided to donate a gold chain worth ₹ 11,000 to the local Ganpati temple. He will pray that this year also goes well.

Gulab had been a student leader in his college at Chiplun, with a dubious background. He had been arrested once and had a police case against himself. He was arrested for siphoning the cash of the student council in his office, some 23,000 rupees in cash. Not only this, but it seemed that Gulab should be quite a character.

He had a case of eve teasing registered against him, but his friend Dhanraj Sonawane, came bustling inside the relevant police station to ensure relevant law was not used. Dhanraj was the younger brother of Kumud Salunkhe, wife of Chief Minister Ajit Salunkhe. Gulab was the son of a police officer who had been suspended for dereliction of duty. He became an alcoholic, but there was no dearth of money in the house as his father Mukund Rao also was notorious for taking bribes. With a snide smile and a wink, he used to say, "My *dukan* (shop) is always open. People just come and drop envelopes in my drawer." Really a man who had no scruples in life. Gulab had imbibed many traits of his father, and lord Ganesha was there, in any case, to help when the chips were down.

Little did he know that the Lord had turned away from him; and that he was about to pay for the sins he had been committing blatantly for the last few years. He thought his proximity and friendship of many years with Dhanraj Sonawane would save him from any wrongdoing if for any reason Ganesha did not act. The two were close friends. Afterall, Dhanraj was the younger brother of Chief Minister Ajit Damodar Salunkhe's wife Kumud, a power centre in her own right. Being the youngest sibling of Kumud's two brothers and three sisters, including her, Dhanraj was a spoilt brat. He had the wrong impression that he was above the law and could get away with anything. He committed crimes blatantly and cared for two hoots for the police or other law enforcement agencies, as the home portfolio was with the CM.

TWENTY-ONE

The police party reached the Vidyalaya along with the two girls. The parole officer asked the girls to point out 'chocolate uncle' if they saw him. She did not know if the girls understood what they had been asked to do. Godambe had a better idea. He asked the Head Master to call all the male workers to line up in front of the girls and see the reaction. But this also did not succeed in getting any reactions from them.

He asked if all workers had come or if some had taken leave. The inspector was told that the Chief Administrative Head, Gulab Rao had taken two days' leave. He had taken his right-hand man, Damu, with him. "Did the Vidyalaya have any photos of the two missing persons? "Yes," said the headmaster. The photos were shown to the girls, and they immediately reacted. They squealed in delight and pointed out to the inspector that Gulab Rao was 'chocolate uncle'. Since he was to join the office in two days, they could only wait.

Just 5 days left for the bye-poll election, and things were already heating up. The exit polls had Nandini winning by just one percentage point. Against the DUS, the much-awaited debate was to be held at the Elphinstone college auditorium at 5 p.m. The debate was to be divided into three halves of 25 minutes each.

Parts 1 and 2 will have each candidate talking about their work and what they will do for the constituency should they win. The candidates can also cross-examine each other in this part of the debate, and part 3 will be taking questions from the public. The moderator was the political science professor from the college.

We had decided that Sitara Chand opt for second place if he won the toss. In my opinion, the words of the person going last are easily remembered as they have been freshly heard. As luck would have it, we won the toss and invited Nandini Kishore to have a go first.

"I am looking forward to finishing the good work my late husband had started. He was loved in this constituency and was re-elected three years ago for a second term as your MLA. I am thankful to the high command for giving me this opportunity to fulfil his legacy and his dreams. I have not been politically inclined, as I think one politician in the family is more than enough. (Her attempt at humour was well received and brought a few chuckles.)

My party has been in power in this state for almost 4 decades, and we have done a lot for our constituents. There is a medical college, two enormous gardens, and an airport that has been approved and will be operational in the next 8/9 months; exclusive schools for girls, good law, and well-maintained order. We are now working on a huge railway junction for up country trains and those going down south, giving us good connectivity.

Eight central government projects have been brought here. You have the branch of the IAS academy, the National Police Training, the Central Branch of AIMS hospital, a branch of the CAG office, a training centre for Naval cadets, and so on. These projects have been brought here to assist our voters. I will not say that if I win since I will win as you will give me a chance to serve you. So after the collector has announced me as the winner, l can assure you that you will be my family. I will make everything possible to make your lives as easy as we can. The CM's wife, Kumud Ji, has assured me of full support and will talk at 4-5 public meetings in the next five days."

A consummate orator, Nandini had put forward her case succinctly and clearly that she would be the winner here. Sitara Chand had been in the public eye for a long time, and he knew the ropes of public speaking. His interpreter was well-versed in the way how Sitara Chand spoke and quickly interpreted what he was saying.

"I think what Nandini ji said was typical of our politicians. It is just rhetoric that she was indulging in. The party she belongs to has been the ruling party for more than 40 years, as she has confessed. What have we achieved in these years? She has not talked about the fact that we have horrible roads. Regarding the state of government hospitals, the state medical college, and municipal schools and corruption rampant in the government departments, some minister or other senior official is under investigation every month for the protection of women. Let me ask her what steps she will take to protect women. Is she willing to distribute the Can for Distress Signals free of cost?"

Nandini did not know where to look, as the high command had not decided on this aspect. The truth was that the amount involved here was huge. The government paid just Rs 250 per Can and sold it, including duty, for Rs 1200. A neat and clear profit of Rs 800 or so per Can, "We are looking into this issue. I am sure we will come up with a solution very soon," she accepted timidly. And has her party done anything for the divyang or the golden senior citizens in the constituency, who were 75 plus in age? Here too, Nandini gave a tame reply. "We will soon announce a committee that will look into this aspect. This reply was neither here nor there.

Anyhow, it was now his turn to speak. Sitara Chand started very confidently. "I am, as you all know, a candidate of the newly formed DUS, which is the party to bring respect to the divyangs in this country. Right from the independence in 1947 till today, we have been marginalised by whichever party ran the centre or state government. We are a strong 8% of the population. Suppose you count the golden senior citizens who are also divyang because of the age factor.

In that case, we are almost 15% of the Indian population, which stands at 140 crores today. That is a huge number, but we do not speak out loud; therefore, we have till now no representation in Lok Sabha or Vidhan Sabha. But that will change from this election onwards since I will be the first from DUS to have fought and won an election. If things had been better and our benefits were as good as those given to the rest of the population, we would not be here fighting to get justice.

Since independence, we have seen that we have got step-motherly treatment. Same horrible roads, the same problem with ramps, no change in problems with railways—I can go on and on. Although we are roughly 15% of the population, we should have got benefits equivalent to the size of 15%. But we hardly had anything done for us. The GST collected in April 2022 was 1.68 lakh crore, and the income tax collected for March 2022 was 12.31 lakh crore. Let us consider that we are only 10% of the population and not 15, as mentioned earlier.

The GST is charged to everyone on whatever you buy or hire, including medicines. Income tax is charged to income over a certain level. So hypothetically speaking, we divyangs have contributed lakhs of crores or at least 10% of the GST and income tax to the national fund, but we have received nothing in return. I am giving you the cold figures as I googled them.

I cannot tell you that I will give you free midday meals, subsidised electricity, or subsidised travel for the Hindu pilgrimage, etc. Since I am not the government, I assure you I will work hard to get you as much benefit as possible. I will fight for public toilets to be installed everywhere, ramps to be compulsory in every building, and trains to have proper and big toilets with immediate effect. And yes, free distribution of the Distress Signals Cans will give lots of protection to all women of India.

The time has come for people with disabilities in India to be given the respect and level playing field in terms of jobs that they want. We do not want to sit at home and twiddle our thumbs. We are as capable as the non-disabled and need a small nudge to go in the right direction. There is a Ministry of Minority Affairs. We demand a ministry for the disabled so that our problems are seen seriously."

Sitara Chand was in his element, and there was utter silence from the goodly crowd as they listened to him with rapt attention. But he concluded at the right time. He had no questions, but the people put Nandini on the mat with several piercing questions.

TWENTY-TWO

Gulab Rao had no idea what awaited him at the Vidyalaya. Sounding cheerful and with a big smile, he entered the premises only to see a police jeep parked near the hostel. Parking his car next to the jeep, he walked towards the hostel to see what it was all about. He thought maybe some boys had a fight and the police were called to control the situation, or maybe a student had tried to commit suicide. Yes, there have been attempts in the past.

At first, he saw the two girls standing with the parole officer to welcome him. Gulab, of course, knew the parole officer who used to come to the hostel regularly. "Chocolate uncle," shouted the girls in unison, happy to see him. "This will be a great night he thought as the girls were in a good mood. And he had plenty of chocolates in his office to keep them happy. He had forgotten to inform Dhanraj about the time of his arrival at the Vidyalaya. Damu will do so. And Dhanraj could bring two of his closest friends, as agreed before he had gone on leave. The girls would not mind as they did not know that the act they had been indulging in, and will again indulge in with Chocolate Uncle and his friends today, was not good.

He sent Damu to his room to bring two chocolates. But as soon as Damu climbed the two steps to reach the lift, two police constables appeared and caught hold of him. Still not alarmed, Gulab Rao asked the constables what they were doing at the Vidyalaya and why they had caught Damu. Suddenly, Sr. Inspector Godambe appeared with handcuffs in his hand." Your game is up. You and your deputy Damu are arrested for repeatedly raping two minor girls."

Godambe then asked the parole officer to call all the girls in the hostel and find out if any other girl has been abused by Gulab Rao. He sent two women constables to help out. Gulab Rao was in tears when they entered the police station. He never thought he would ever be caught. The girls would not talk as they did not understand what was happening. They were just happy with their chocolates. And Damu, willing to participate in the sexual abuse of the two girls, would never open his mouth. That left Dhanraj and some friends he brought now and then, and they would have no reason to talk to or call the police. So, Gulab Rao was confused.

He returned to reality when Godambe snapped his fingers before his face. "I am shocked at the crime you have committed. These children need shelter from the wicked world outside. They need your protection, but you and Damu betrayed their trust. I am appalled at what you have done. If it is left to me, I will shoot you; but even if I desperately want to, I can't do so.

It is because we have law and order and must follow certain procedures. Do you know when you go to prison, which is the most hated crime? Which even the most hardened criminals hate? It is a crime against children. So, what do you think will happen to you? There will be a line of criminals, all sex-starved, who will be impatient to sodomise you. It will be harrowing and may run into many months. Plus, the humiliation attached to it."

Late at night, an exhausted parole officer went to the police station to tell Godambe what she had found out from other girls and make a report as an FIR because the mentally challenged could not make or sign the report.

"What I have found out is extremely shocking and disgusting. Many girls came forward to complain about Gulab Rao's behaviour. He seems to be a sex maniac and has been doing this for many years. I have a written and signed statement by six other girls, and now I will give you the most shocking news.

Four teenage boys were also survivors as they were raped, but the fear of Gulab Rao was so evident and apparent that even the headmaster knew about this but did not have the guts to challenge Gulab Rao. I think the headmaster is also guilty as an accessory, as he knew a disturbing and heinous crime was being conducted in his Vidyalaya against minor children. He never went to the police to complain about what was happening."

Godambe had not said a word during this outburst by the officer, but internally, he was boiling with anger. "Did he have any outsiders coming in to abuse the children? Some friends of his—"

"I am coming to that. It seems there was one constant friend and a few others. They would have drinks first, make the girls drink with them, and then ask them to remove their clothes and commit rape. And guess who is the constant friend of Gulab Rao? The Headmaster, who is in the docks anyway, finally gave up the name.

"It is Dhanraj, the younger brother of the Chief Minister's wife, Kumud. The kids also said that Dhanraj was also 'chocolate uncle'. In effect, he was the brother-in-law of the powerful CM. Dhanraj is very close to the power centre."

Godambe sighed deeply. There were going to be a lot of problems, and this would be a late night for him as there were many problems. Many complications as far as this case was concerned. He knew the case had to be kept under the wrappers as the media would have a field day with this one. But it was almost impossible to do so. And with just five days to go for the important bye-election, this case could be the factor that will decide the fate of the result.

TWENTY-THREE

As far as we were concerned, we knew this was a death knell for Nandini Kishore. We had to milk it as much as possible for us. Besides, as Godambe had felt and had predicted, the media got a whiff of the sensational news, and so did we, as some journalist friends called to inform us what had happened and that the name of Dhanraj was being thrown about as a perpetrator and as a sex hound. I immediately called for a party meeting when they trooped in and briefed my friends.

"This is good news for us. We have to use it judiciously. The CM must have known by now of this drastic and dirty crime. I guess they will pressure the police to go slow on this. The parole officer has already filed the FIR in the evening. So, the ruling party cannot do much about it. Let's see what happens in the morning when the story hits out at the CM."

Dhanraj Sonawane was hiding, and the police did not know where to start. They wanted to talk to his sister Kumud Salunkhe, but she could not be contacted. Her phones were switched off, which was expected, but Godambe posted two constables outside the CM's residence just in case.

Ajit Damodar Salunkhe was in his second term as Chief

Minister. He was hard-working and fully conscious of his duties as CM. He had the confidence of the high command. He had a pretty strong grip on the law and order of his state and had kept the home department under him. He could not contain the devil of corruption; he also had made a fair amount of cash by now, which was to be used when it mattered. He was married to Kumud, a very ambitious woman whose sight was on a ministry in the centre after this term here was over. But her one weakness was her indulgence in her younger brother, Dhanraj. She saw no evil in him and was prepared to overlook all his misdeeds. She was extremely fond of him.

Ajit Salunkhe was briefed by the Police Commissioner just as he sat down for dinner. The Commissioner told him what had happened and that it was grave. Dhanraj is in hiding and has switched off his phone. He is also wanted for a DNA test as one of the girls is pregnant. Fuming angrily, the CM immediately called for his wife and a full cabinet meeting within the hour. Kumud got the summons, and she hurried to see what he wanted, though she knew exactly what he had called her for.

Dhanraj had called her soon after he got a call from a peon from the Vidyalaya who was on his payroll. She instructed him to leave the city, go to her village, and stay with their family friends, who had a huge farm with many places to hide. He was to stay put till he got a call from her. Ajit was red on his face as he confronted her. "What is this brother of yours up to? I had told you before to put him on a leash, and it bothers me that you didn't listen. Now he has gone and committed the worst crime possible—" Kumud cut him off, saying, "He has made a mistake. He will repent and not do these things again. He has promised me. He was with some friends and took advantage of these girls several times, I know. So, you can tell the Police Commissioner to go easy on Dhanraj."

A perplexed Ajit wanted to know what exactly the brother had told her. Just that he got carried away after a few drinks, she said. Roared Ajit, "He has made a girl pregnant, and she is mentally challenged. Do you know what the media will do to me? TV reports will soon be breaking news where I will be crumpled; print media will kill me tomorrow, and I have an election to win. I am having three public meetings before the poll day. What will I say? Where is he now? Don't hide him. If the media knows you helped hide him. My political career will be finished. Have you thought about this? You are blind in your love for him." He stomped out, going to the cabinet room where ministers were assembling.

I was contacted by a TV reporter late in the night. He wanted to know the stance of DUS if Dhanraj was found to be involved in the rape of these innocent girls. "It is horrible what these men were up to. I understand the police have detained him; this is the most evil crime I have encountered. These two girls are mentally challenged; they do not realise what they did was wrong.

Imagine they allowed these *haramjade lafanges* (bastard loafers) to take advantage of them. These perpetrators should be hanged as they knew the girls had problems." The next question was if I thought that the CM's brother-in-law was evading the police. "Yes, of course. CM also looks after the home department. He has to be aware of where Dhanraj is. If it is proved that he knew that, too. He must be questioned. He may be an accessory to the crime and should be jailed." These are harsh words," said the reporter. But I went further and said, "Since the criminal was Kumud Salunkhe's brother, she may well be the one who knew from the beginning where he was hiding. Then, if proved, she also must be jailed."

I was aware that my statements caused *hungama* (ruckus) the next day. But I slept well that night, sensing a big victory in the bye-elections. The atmosphere in cabinet meetings was tense. Chairing it, Ajit said, we have a major problem. There have been several rapes in the government-run Vidyalaya for mentally challenged orphans.

It happened for several months, and one of the girls was pregnant. So, what can we do?" But there had been a power tussle in the party some months ago. The CM could barely save his seat because of the revolt of three ministers. One immediately came to the point, knowing it would hurt the CM.

"There are rumours that your wife's brother is the leader of the criminals who raped the two unfortunate girls. What are you going to do about it? "If I come to find out where he is hiding, I will get him arrested. You be rest assured," answered the CM. The cabinet decided to wait after seeing how the media played out this episode the next morning.

TWENTY-FOUR

5 Days Left for Voting

The TV played right through the night the report of the rapes in the Vidyalaya, a state government-run institution. My statements on the CM and his wife were headline stuff, as I had asked them to be jailed, but the newspapers had catchy and bold headlines.

"CM on a falling wicket. Brother-in-law raped mentally challenged girls for months".

"I demand jail for CM and wife, says Sanjay Sharma of DUS."

"Government institutions can't protect our girls."

"Does Kumud know where her darling brother is hiding?"

"CM should resign immediately and clear his name before returning to the chair."

"Death penalty for the serial rapists screamed the Women's Group."

"Dhanraj is required for a DNA test. Where is he hiding?"

So on and so forth. There was chaos all over. The CM was upset about my demand that he should be jailed, along with Kumud; livid with anger, he summoned the Police Commissioner. He also asked Commerce Minister Damle, a real loyalist, to join him immediately.

"What the hell is going on? This bastard Dhanraj had been going to the Vidyalaya for several months, and you had no clue about this. What sort of intelligence network are you running? You should be ashamed of yourself. I am giving you 24 hours. Find him or put your resignation on my desk." He dismissed the hassled Commissioner. Deepak Damle came in to find the CM in a foul mood. "Who is this? Sanjay Sharma suggested that Kumud and I should be jailed.

Why is he baying for my blood? Is he the same fellow with whom you skirmished last month over that Distress Signal Can issue?" "Yes," said Deepak, "He is the same person, very arrogant and full of vanity. He thinks no end of himself. He wanted to push me into a corner over the issue. He has started the Divyang Unnati Sangthan. Empowerment of the divyang is the main motto. He is a former international badminton player with many friends in the media. Not to be taken lightly. He does his homework."

"Yes, I see. So what is happening to that issue of the Signals?"

"I am trying to postpone it as much as possible. Giving it free of cost will hit our finances deeply. We can't afford to do this. But we have to come out with a strategy to counter them." The CM, persisting with the Signals issue, said, "It was a very clever move on their part. We will have to toe their line and provide it free of cost. Sooner, the better. I have asked the high command to let us know what to do about it. Keep an eye on him and the DUS. He can be dangerous."

Sitara Chand Gopal could feel slowly that more and more people were coming to hear him in the public rallies. The tide was slowly turning against the ruling party with four days to go for voting. But anything can happen in an election, as many promises are made at election time. And that is what happened. The Prime

Minister announced that education be free for all females. Previously, free education was announced for girls in the upper classes. But with the new gift to girls, education was free from the first standard.

The party had designed the offer craftily, as it did not break any election rules. Some fifteen days before the elections, the incumbent government cannot offer free goodies. This free education was for girls all over the country. This hit a chord with female voters; they all appreciated the offer.

The police ran around to find out where Dhanraj was hiding. A team headed by an ACP was dispatched to the native village of Kumud on a tip that he could be hiding there. Gulab Rao and Damu were grilled every two hours. They were not allowed to sleep or given water. How many of them had been in this gang? What was the role of Dhanraj? Who had started it? They were grilled together and also separately.

Where was Dhanraj hiding? Godambe had strict orders from the Commissioner himself. Gulab Rao was very close to Dhanraj. He should have some idea. Break him by tonight. Use any method. Gulab Rao knew that Dhanraj would flay him if he escaped this carnage. He was a tough nut to crack, but Godambe had an idea.

In the meantime, the six other girls who were also abused were asked by the police to make a statement describing what had happened to them and who the culprits were. Can they pick them out from a group of dirty and *gunda* (gangster) type-looking line ups? The boys who had been victimised and abused also were going to make a statement. Since they were all juveniles under 18, their names could not be revealed. So, the parole officer signed the statement on behalf of the girls, and Inspector Godambe signed for the boys.

As the day wore on, the media became restless. The CM and

Kumud were not speaking to anyone. I was getting call after call to say something, anything they said. I was becoming a good copy. I agreed to talk to a bunch of TV reporters. Instant breaking news was the call of the day. So, my talk with them will be breaking news within an hour. In any case, I had nothing to lose. "It looks like DUS will win the bye poll. What will you ask for from the government in case you win? I realised that my answers to them keep us in the national conscience for days to come."

The DUS will not demand anything. All we want is for our rights to be upheld and for us divyangs to be given what has been due to us for decades. But yes, we demand that the Distress Signal issue be brought up front and a decision be taken by the government immediately. They are side tracking it for no reason. Then I strongly feel that all divyangs who are not able to work due to their disability should be given a monthly stipend by the government. How else can they survive? The ones who work but require 24/7 helpers and physiotherapy, medicines, etc., should not be asked to pay any tax." I told them these are some of our requests to the government.

There were many other questions relating to the bye-election, but they were mundane. Except for this question I was waiting for, I had given them enough to be happy for 24 hours.

"The state says they hardly have any funds. So how will you supply free Distress Signals to our women for their safety?" I answered by saying that the state had enough resources. "Don't believe them. I said," They are spending crores in taking out full-page adverts in leading newspapers monthly. Then there are these ugly hoardings all over the town, their leaders looking down on us with a benevolent smile, telling us how much work they have done for us citizens."

But dear reader, this is their job; this is what we have voted them for. Public transport is also not spared. The city buses carry messages, and so does the Metro Network. So, if the government stops this nonsense, they will be shocked at how much money the state is left with. It will be difficult to spend that cash." During my travels abroad, I have never seen hoardings of political leaders or full-page ads in the media. Why we do it in India escapes me.

The Police Commissioner sought an appointment with the CM. "Sir," started the policeman, "We need to question Madam Kumud, as she is the closest to the fugitive. She can throw light on his whereabouts." Knowing that the situation was dicey, Ajit Salunkhe had to agree to Commissioner's request. Kumud did not give straightforward answers but reluctantly allowed the police search party to visit her village and question family and friends. But she did not accept that she knew the whereabouts of Dhanraj. When asked when she last spoke to her dear brother, she kept evading the answer. Finally, she hid behind. "I can't remember when I talked to him. "

Godambe brought a couple of detainees to the next cell to make Gulab Rao talk and started the third degree with them. The screams of the detainees reverberated all over the police station as Godambe hit them with his stick and slapped them around. This brought a chill in the stomach of Gulab Rao and Damu. But first, they were told to stand in line with 4 others for the identification parade. One by one, the abused children were brought in, and they all pointed to Gulab Rao and Damu as persons who had abused them. The case against these two was now airtight, fool proof; they could not escape the wrath of justice.

The rest of the day went on as everyone was busy doing their work or what was allotted.

TWENTY-FIVE

Four Days Left for Voting

The next day, CM was to hold two public rallies in the constituency.

My requests for benefits for people with disabilities was the day's topic; it was being debated all over the state. Every single divyang, whatever their disability, hailed me as a messiah. Sitara Chand was thankful to me as people with disabilities in the constituency hailed it as an eye-opener and game changer for them.

Godambe shifted Gulab and Damu to the interrogation cell. The cell smelt of sweat and fear and reeked of urine; many a culprit, waiting for his date in the court, was given a third-degree welcome. And during the interrogation, he empties his bladder of fear. Gulab and Damu did not protest much. A couple of slaps, each with full force, had them babbling. "They did not know where exactly Dhanraj was hiding, but he had told them a few times about a family friend's farm in his village. He used to have consensual sex with the wife of the *mali* (gardener) in the barn which housed the cows.

Kalyani, the gardener's wife, was also cleaning the main farm building along with the barn. This is the place where Dhanraj has been hiding for the last three days. She did not know who he was as she was illiterate and could not read the local newspaper. She was a typical village belle who did her job dutifully and did not loiter around for no reason. Her world was her husband, Maruti. They had been married for just five months. Kalyani had a lovely figure and an innocence about her.

When she went to clean the barn, Dhanraj was there but did not try anything unwanted. But she sensed evil around the man who followed her with a lecherous graze.

But she was uneasy while she was cleaning the barn. Completing her work, she moved out fast. The next day when she went to the barn, he started making lewd gestures, making it apparent what he wanted.

When she did not respond, he brought out a handful of rupees to show he was willing to pay a good amount of cash. Clearly alarmed now, Kalyani sprinted out of the barn.

She mulled then over than the fact whether she should complain to Maruti. Maruti, a strong and well-muscled youngster, ran the local *akhara* (gym). He was short-tempered, and on her complaint, he would surely drag Dhanraj and break a few bones. Kalyani thought that she should give them one more day at the barn and see if the man could be told to mind his life. But she saw that a police van was parked outside, and as she watched, she saw two hefty constables who pushed Dhanraj, catching him by the collar and pushing him inside the van. With a sigh of relief, and calmly walked into the barn.

Inside the barn is a small, well-hidden room, and the door is difficult to see. In this room, Dhanraj used to boast that he regularly had females joining him. The room is pretty isolated, and the barn is far from the main road. Dhanraj had invited Gulab to come and have a good time in his village. Gulab was keen to go, but the ecstasy trip somehow never manifested.

Godambe, with his experience of interrogation, knew that he had been told the truth by these two. He promptly called the Commissioner with the news and got the police party to go to this barn.

Around 6 p.m., I had another date with the media in the evening. This time over 60 were present, covering every single major TV station or print media. Today, of course, TV carried a lot of stories on me. They had dug the ground to find out my last playing days. How was I, as a shuttler? How was my married life? How did I become a divyang? and how did I come to lead the community in this by-poll?

"That is all good, Sanjay Ji, but what drastic changes must the government make to get the disabled on a level playing field?" A fair question, I thought. "I strongly feel that there should have been a ministry of the divyangs with a dedicated Minister who would have ensured that we got fruits for our labour. There has been Ministry for minority affairs for so many years. They look after the minorities' interests. Then there is a ministry for tribal welfare. We have been a strong 15% of the population.

Yet, we got nothing in return for the loyalty we have shown to this ruling party roughly for the last 50 years." The next question was also interesting. "Are you going to join politics in the future? You seem to be very popular with the *janta*."

This stumped me. Was I interested in joining politics? I don't know, but it has been exciting so far. "I have not given it a thought. I had joined my two friends Satya Prakash Tiwari and Rajaram Ghag, in their quest to get justice for Fazil and Ahmed Hussain, the two polio inflicted who were denied using the lift in their college. I am not saying no for the simple reason that I have not given it a thought. I will surely let you know once I decide."

The police search party hit the jackpot at the barn. They had been well briefed. The police also took the family friend in custody as he was hiding the fugitive. The Commissioner was informed. He was also informed that they had taken the phone of Dhanraj in custody and were going through his recent calls. The village was some 159 km away, so it took approximately 4 to 5 hours to reach the police station where Godambe was situated.

The first rally of CMS Ajit Salunkhe had only 200 to 250 persons attending. And most of these were bussed in from nearby villages at the party's expense. They were here because they were promised ₹ 500 each and a small *daru* (liquor) bottle; this was fiesta time for the fans. The second meeting was better since the CM talked about the freebies government and had doled out to the electorate. "We will continue giving you freebies so you don't have to pay anything. All you have to do is to vote for Nandini Kishore."

As he descended from the stage to go to his office, someone shouted from the crowd, *"Ajit bhau tumhare biwi par tumko control nahin hai to is prant par kaise control karoge? Tum ko to Dhanraj ke bare mein malum ho na ho Kumud ko pucca malum hai. Tum to Gaye—"* (Ajit brother, you do not have any control over your wife, how are you going to control this state?)—The crowd started to boo him.

Ajit was too stunned to say anything; he walked fast to reach his official car and was swiftly whisked away by his security. He called for the cabinet meeting, but before that, he wanted a quick word with Deepak Damle, who had rushed to the CM residence, reaching before the boss. The news of the CM being booed went viral, but his woes were not over yet. He was going to be hit by a Tsunami very soon.

Godambe was getting impatient waiting for the police party with Dhanraj. He wanted to stand him up for identification from the kids. Once confirmed that Dhanraj was the main perpetrator, the case was wrapped up as far as he was concerned. What they did politically was not his concern. He had done his job by providing this case's crucial link and potential breakthrough, but he had no choice except to wait.

The CM alighted from his car and summoned Damle to follow him.

"I don't know what is happening, Deepak, but I think I am losing control over the government. I was booed today in my election meeting. Then the police chief caught, Dhanraj, and they got this goonda to the city in the next two hours. And I do not have a good feeling about him. God knows what he will say at the police station, where he will be questioned. Then you know, I have this peculiar feeling that the media is getting help from someone.

Otherwise, how are they so informed about what we may do next?" Damle said that it had to be me, Sanjay Sharma, who was feeding the media, as many there were my friends. "Then control him and help me. Use any method but make sure he remains silent until the polling day. Just 3 days more. Can I depend on you?" The CM enquired. "Sir," said Damle, "I will do my very best to do what you want. The police caravan reached the destination within the allotted time, and Dhanraj has whisked away for the identification line-up. The media vans were outside waiting for the news from inside.

The identification was just a waste of time since as soon as the abused kids saw Dhanraj, they jumped up and pointed at him; Godambe did not want to take any chances and had a full line-up per the system. The identification was done, and the DNA report was only pending. And, of course, he had to find out what Kumud had discussed with Dhanraj regarding the hiding place on the farm.

Since he did not have his phone, he had no idea what Kumud

had been up-to. He had been interrogated, and had she disclosed anything tonight to the police under pressure? And, of course, the friend from the village who owned the farm also had to be detained.

TWENTY-SIX

Three Days Left for Voting

At 9:25 pm, the Police Commissioner came out with a smug smile on his face. The waiting media pounced on him. "What have you got on Dhanraj? Is he also going to be arrested with Gulab Rao and Damu? Has his DNA report also come? Is Kumud also going to be arrested for knowing where he was hiding? The questions come in a cascade." "I cannot tell you what is in the reports, but we have his DNA and identification reports. I am now going to CM residence where the CM will decide what to do further." Pointed out the Commissioner. A huge crowd had almost gheraoed the residence.

The Commissioner met the CM and came straight to the point. "Sir, I have the DNA report of the accused and fugitive Dhanraj. The kids identified him. He had sexually abused them, and the DNA is positive. His residual semen was also found on the girl who was pregnant. So, he has been arrested, and we will take these criminals to the special court for the juvenile in the morning. And Sir, I have bad news for you. We recovered the accused's mobile phone; two phone calls are very important. He got a call from a peon of the Vidyalaya, and then he called up your wife, and they talked for two minutes. I am afraid she lied to us. It is my job to give you the correct information that we have unearthed. It is up to you how to use it."

There was a pin-drop silence as the CM digested the news. The baby had been dropped in his lap, hook, line, and sinker. He immediately called for Kumud and confronted her over the news from the Police Commissioner. "Your brother has almost finished me politically. He is in police custody and has yet to give information.

Believe me, once the police start using the third degree, he will sing like a canary. He will name you as the one person he contacted, and you suggested that he should hide in that barn; his DNA has tested positive as his residual semen was found on the girl whom he made pregnant. I have never liked that fellow, but you always insisted I go easy on him. Well, there you are. You decide what is to be done. Now meet the Commissioner you lied to; he is waiting in the other room, and see what can be done."

The cabinet meeting was stormy with flaying tempers. Through their sources, most of the ministers had already seen the report. They knew that Dhanraj would go behind bars for a long time. But what about Kumud? Will she get the benefit of the doubt, or will she also be arrested? The night was going to be deadly in every way. There was not much pressure in the morning, but build-up had started for an interesting night. Though the main interest now was whether Kumud was to be arrested, small bytes about the Vidyalaya and how it became a den for sexual activities were awaited. The headmaster, who knew what was happening and did not inform the police that under 18 years old kids were being subjected to carnal activities, was also arrested.

Kumud knew she was under a lot of suspicion from everyone, but she thought of contacting her lawyer Ayaz Bilawala and rang him up, but Ayaz was busy playing at a badminton event. However serious, seeing many missed calls from the CM's wife, he realised something was wrong. He knew what it could be as he read the newspapers daily and was fully glued to the information that he imbibed from the media.

So, he decided to go directly to the CM's residence. Kumud told him to come by the back entrance so that the hordes of journalists who were at the entry did not come to know that she had called for her lawyer. She met Ayaz at the back gate and immediately blurted out, "What can you do to save me, Ayaz? I have got into a mess. I don't know what to do. I do not want to go to jail—Ayaz calmed her down and asked, "Tell me, when did you come to know Dhanraj is involved? After his phone call or before, let us say after. Does anyone says otherwise? Did anyone hear you talking to him? Nobody. Now let us see the facts. The fact is that he called. The fact is you spoke to him for approximately two minutes.

These two facts cannot be denied because the police have the records. But you can deny that you spoke to him about the farm or where he should hide. I do not think they can do anything to you. They do not have any proof. So, you need not worry. Just maintain what we have discussed. Even if they try to make a fool of you, just do not react and just maintain your stand, but do not interfere with the working of the police."

The CM Ajit Salunkhe, however, would not have it easy. The three rebels in the cabinet openly asked for his resignation on the pretext that the CM's family was shaming him and, thereby, the CM chair. Ajit, however, said that he had not interfered in any investigation on his wife or brother-in-law. He said he would be happy if both were acquitted, but if they have to follow the law, he is ready to make sure they pass the acid test. He had called a press conference late at night, at 11 p.m., to answer charges of the media. Time left for a quick dinner, and in the brief chat with Kumud, he came to know what Ayaz Bilawala, her advocate, had deduced.

Feeling better, he met the press to answer the charges against the family. The questions came in a torrent, and he had to be careful with his answers.

Q: What do you have to say about the behaviour of Dhanraj?

A: I am appalled at the way he has gone about and abused these children. I hope he gets the maximum penalty.

Q: You have always said the state has a good law and order record. How, then, did you not know what was happening at the Vidyalaya?

A: I am sincerely sorry that what happened at the Vidyalaya is an aberration and will not happen again.

Q: Then again, how can we take your word for it? Especially because your family was involved in this rape episode?

A: You have to take my word for it. In any case, Dhanraj is not my family. Kumud is, and she has done no wrong.

This upped the antenna of the media.

Q: How can you say that when still Dhanraj and the friend from their village have not been interrogated regarding her role?

A: CM was alarmed by this as he had not factored in interrogating these two, but he had to say something. "Of course, we will wait for the interrogation to be completed. Why don't we meet tomorrow at 10 am? By that time, the questioning will be over."

TWENTY-SEVEN

Two Days Left for Voting

The interrogation of Dhanraj and his friend started in two different cells at about 12:30 a.m. Inspector Godambe handled Dhanraj while Inspector Gaekwad had to question the friend. The Commissioner had said to use any method but get the information. "I want to show this CM that he can't take the police force for granted. He shouts and abuses senior officials in public also. I need something on Kumud. Get me a signed confession from both." He told the two inspectors.

Godambe and Gaekwad were experts in not leaving a mark on the body, so the criminals couldn't tell the court that the police had beaten them up to get a confession. The police inspectors went to work after explaining to them what was going to happen. So, they have a choice of either accepting that Kumud knew the hiding place of Dhanraj and escaping the beating they will get now. Or don't accept but explain to the two police inspectors that you would break within 30 minutes guaranteed.

As expected, the family friend from the village was first to break.

A dozen slaps, followed by just 10 cane hits on his backside, did the trick. Crying loudly—he was willing to sign anything. He said, "Kumud had called me saying that Dhanraj had trouble and required hiding in some place for a couple of days. How could I say no to her? She is the wife of the CM, very powerful in her own right. When Dhanraj came, I gave him the door to the barn and told him I would get some food and water. Sir, believe me, I had no choice. If I had known he had committed such a heinous crime, I would never have agreed to Kumud at all."

In the other cell, Dhanraj took some time to come around. He still thought the elder sister would come, accompanied by the CM, would walk in any moment, and this nightmare would end. After all, she saved him many times, always forgiving his misdemeanours; but that did not happen, and in about 20 minutes, he cracked. He could have sustained some more physical beating.

Still, when Godambe told him that an electric shock would be next to his testicles, he knew it was time to accept that he did receive her advice to hide on the farm. "I called her. I was really worried about what would happen once the police caught me, but she said you can't hide here in the city. She said the old barn at the farm would be ideal."

He signed the confession.

The Commissioner had said, "Whatever time they sign the confession, you must bring it to me. I will take it to the CM. I will love that I wake him up at an ungodly hour. Like he does to us." He had a sinister smile on his face. "And don't forget that exactly one hour from now, you both will tell your sources in the media that Kumud will be arrested for misleading the police and helping a fugitive from the law."

With spring in his walk now, as he sprinted the steps to the CM's office, he asked the guard on duty to wake the CM. As he had some major news to give. The surprised guard was not sure now what to do. He looked at his watch and looked doubtful, "Sir, at this time?" "Yes," thundered the Commissioner. Do it now. Immediately.

A groggy-eyed CM came out, not happy at all at this incursion. "Commissioner, the news better be important. Let's have it." The news is not good, Sir. Both Dhanraj and the other guy have signed a statement implicating your wife. I am afraid she was instrumental in hiding him. It is now a police case. I have brought it to you first so you can decide what to do with this news." He saluted and left.

Ajit Salunkhe was stunned by her stupidity and was now in this mess. But he was to get deeper and deeper into this quagmire with no exit.

3 AM

I got a call from one of the newspaper columnists in a major media house. "Have you heard the latest?" he asked. "What can be so important that you wake me up at 3 a.m?" He chuckled," You will forget the sleep when you hear what I say. I was *maha* curious now. Sleep vanished when he said, "CM's wife Kumud had been in touch with Dhanraj and helped him hide in her village. The two in police custody have a signed confession implicating her in this sordid mess.

It is only a matter of time before she is arrested for abetting and helping a fugitive on the run.

I was fully awake now, devising a strategy to give good mileage to the cause of DUS. I called my team, telling them what had happened and what we should do now. I had a plan in my head, and I asked them if they could rustle up some volunteers, about thirty to forty, for a *dharna* to be held at the CM office/residence in exactly one hour. In unison, they said they would get on the job immediately. I asked them to assemble at the venue by 4 a.m. Ravin meticulously maintained a register with all volunteer party members' names, addresses, and mobile numbers. He ticked off the first fifty names and was glad all fifty agreed. Such was the enthusiasm in the party. It bodes well for the future of DUS, he thought.

I was amazed to see that some volunteers had already reached. There was a smattering of media people, too, but surely this place would soon be packed as this was huge news within the media circle, and it had spread fast. My team also arrived, and I briefed them on what must be done. I had my trusted megaphone with me. All that we had to do was to scream *hai hai* after I yelled "Kumud Salunkhe." In short, we were to make a nuisance of ourselves. One *chowkidar* (watchman) taking his rounds saw all of us, but when told we were the media, he said, "Fine, carry on." He had seen worse crowds here.

Inside the residence, the atmosphere was cold and deadly. With Ajit not acknowledging the presence of Kumud and the wife pouting away to glory, it was left to Damle to broker peace between them. CM had already called him for talks. I saw him coming when a car screeched to a halt beside me. He was alarmed to see so many of us already assembled there when the time given to them was 10 a.m. "What are you doing here? You can't have *dharna* as here it is illegal to assemble in such large numbers at CM residence." He rushed in ostensibly to do our *chugli* (badmouth) but found that the CM was already aware of media build-up. However, he had, it seems, no idea that DUS was already here.

"Damle, what is happening outside? You must be aware that the test reports of the two culprits have come positive, and they have also been in touch with Kumud, who guided them on where to hide, etc. She is in big trouble, and I cannot do anything about it as there is so much focus on this case, but I have to do something about her even though she has done something stupid. I don't want to become a laughing stock and come to be known as the 'CM who could not control his wife; how can he control a state?' My career would be over. I don't care about Dhanraj or the other fellow. So what do you think I should do." The media was piling up, and at sharp 6, they would be filing their report.

"Sir, you should ask the advocate Ayaz Bilawala to file for anticipatory bail immediately. Though the Court will be closed now, a night judge is always designated to take action for emergencies. Anything connected with you is urgent if you so desire. So, call Ayaz right now, and you come out to meet the media only when the bail document is in our hands. Not before."

At 6 a.m., people outside began to stir as they were getting impatient and wanted to get this over with. But the CM was not to be seen. No one knew what time he would show his face. Damle came out and jumped in his car, and went off in a hurry. He would meet Ayaz, who was due to reach the court soon. My volunteers were getting restless with nothing to do. Amrita then asked me what we should do. Our patience was being tested, no doubt, but I had assembled them at a very unusual hour for protest. So, I better come good and start something.

I decided we should hit on Kumud, the weak link in this story, and keep up the pressure on the CM to take action against her. We did not realise that behind the scene, games were on and that anticipatory bail was being sought. I started on the megaphone yelling, "Kumud Salunkhe," the DUS shouted in unison, "*hai hai*," which continued for almost half an hour. Then a break of ten minutes. During this interval, some TV reporters started their cameras, and suddenly we were on national TV 'live' again. "Kumud Salunkhe *hai hai*" reverberated all over, shattering the early morning calm. The TV crews suddenly started activating my senior team for interviews on live national TV. I had wanted Satya, Rajaram, Amrita, Hamid, and Ravin to share the national limelight. It was DUS all over from 6-8 a.m., stirring the nation's consciousness.

There was no response from the residence till 8 a.m. when Damle came rushing in. The CM then came out, escorted by Damle. The media went silent, and we wondered what he had to say. "I have good news. Both the accused have confessed to the crime. The law will deal with them." "However, what about your wife?" someone shouted. "Yes, yes, I am coming up to that. There is confusion about whether she knew about Dhanraj being arrested, So I am clearing the air. Of course, she knew, but whether she also told him where to hide was another matter. Since she has anticipatory bail, she must clear her name as early as possible."

We all waiting outside the residence were shocked that they had filed for bail in the middle of the night and got it. It smacked of fear, deep fear. "She got bail, but how?" Everyone present found this difficult to believe. Then they got vociferous, each one screaming away at the top of their voices, increasing the cacophony to high decibels. "Is Kumud guilty or not?" That was the question.

"I cannot tell you anything as the matter now is subjudice." Claimed the CM. But in your opinion, is she guilty or not is what we want to know. But the CM was not going to budge from his position. I felt insulted that he was trying to camouflage such a blatant lie. My DUS team was getting impatient. I consulted with some TV crew and continued our *dharna* for at least two more hours. So, it was back to the megaphone and Kumud Salunkhe *hai hai*, at the top of our voices.

TWENTY-EIGHT

9.30 AM

At 9.30, Damle came bustling outside, straight to me. In a very condescending tone, he roared, "Sharma, I told you no *dharna* here. It is prohibited, as you can see the sign on that post. Assembly of more than six persons cannot occur, so pack your stuff and get out of here, or I will call the police." "We will leave in an hour. Till then, we are staying put. We have a right to demonstrate since the CM is not being fair. Everyone knows that Kumud is guilty. Why is he shielding her?" I asked Damle, but he was in no mood to listen. So let them evict us, but we will continue without fear, I told my team.

"Kumud Salunkhe hai hai," thundered the DUS on again and again.

True to his word, Damle called for the police to evict us.

Sirens blazing and lights flashing, two vans came bustling down to us, and a Sr Inspector jumped out of the first van and came to me, "Please stop this right now and leave. What you are doing is prohibited here as this is a sensitive area.' We are demonstrating peacefully, I told him. The CM is not allowing us to meet Kumud Salunkhe, who should have been arrested by now. So, till she comes out to answer our questions, we will not move from here."

The TV crew, who had not left, started to film our face-off. Damle called the inspector, and major whispering started between them. At the same time, we continued with our slogans, loud and clear at the top of our voices. There were some 15 policemen against 50 of us divyangs. But in his team, only 5 women constables were present. At the same time, we had 23 females with us.

The inspector said, "You all have to leave immediately. I don't want to use force, but if forced, I will." He was already on his mobile calling for reinforcement. "You have to be joking," I said under my breath. The country will be in flames if they see scenes of police atrocity against people with disabilities. I said loudly, mainly aiming the missile at Damle, " You dare not use force against us. You will become a laughing stock." But Damle was adamant that we had to be evicted.

The reinforcement brought together another 15 police personnel and slowly formed a ring around us. Now, people with disabilities take much more time than the non-disabled. Callipers, crutches, and wheelchairs are just aids to get you around. But what took me, for example, ten seconds to walk to any destination when I could, now it takes me around sixty to seventy-odd seconds. With callipers, it will be much more.

In my Divyang group, I had a mix of wheelchair users, calliper users, crutch users, canes for visually impaired people, and elbow support users. As the police tightened the ring around us, my team panicked. In their eagerness to get away from the advancing police line, a few fell, and this caused a small stampede in which ten others toppled.

Amrita, who was encouraging the second line of DUS to come forward, found herself in the middle of her group. But since there was no movement in front because of the mini stampede, the persons not hurt were pushing back; and the group behind was pushing the ones in front. And in that classic pincer movement where there was no respite, Amrita's group was being crushed front and back.

In the melee, one girl from the first group fell; the others tried to stop but could not; and two others piled on top of the first girl who was being crushed, and she, also being an asthma patient, started to get choked, and became unconscious. Amrita, in the meantime, was in the centre of group 2, felt the pressure from all sides, and could not stop herself from falling. Unfortunately, her head hit a stone, and she started to ooze blood. Persons behind her saw blood and started screaming for an ambulance.

I had reached where we had the girl who had fainted due to an asthma scare as she had choked and Amrita, who was bleeding from the cut on the head. An ambulance had to be called as both needed immediate attention from a doctor. Amrita refused to go as she said, "We are doing this for a great cause. I will not go to the Hospital. I will continue to support this movement.

As if to reassure us that she was in her senses, she screamed Kumud Salunkhe *hai hai*, and all others responded in chorus. That was the spirit we had, somehow inculcated in the DUS. We kept clashing with the police, but no one wanted to stop or withdraw. There were screams of pain, despair, of helplessness, but even when Damle ordered more police, my team continued to fight.

All realised this was a huge moment for us as national TV was filming and reporting live to a shocked nation. The breaking news on every channel was DUS fighting for justice and the cruel police attacking divyangs literally. Amrita, with her bleeding head, was the heroine as well as the picture of the day.

I found Damle and asked him to stop this action as my people were getting hurt. "I will not ask the police to stop till your people halt the crazy slogan they have," he said with a sneer. "But we are holding a peaceful *dharna* and should be allowed to carry on." However, he was in no mood to relent. Then he said something which was hitting us below the belt.

"You people live on the sympathy of the non-disabled people. What would you be if not for us? Yet, you want free distress signals, don't want to pay tax, free this and free that. You don't request; you demand. Let me tell you that whatever you do, you are nothing. You have no power." When his rant was over, I told him point blank, "Damle, you are vain and arrogant; power has gone into your head. We have requested only and waited from 1947. We were timid, vulnerable, and helpless. However, no more. Democracy has given us the same rights as you; we will exercise these rights now. You will see. You will see the Power of Divyang."

4 PM

I called the team for an urgent meeting at 4 pm and told them what Damle had said to me word for word. It angered them so much that they wanted to take revenge immediately. We have to make Damle grovel. But how do we do it? We all gave it serious thought and tried to conclude. Ravin came up with an idea that appealed to all of us. Ravin said, "The administration did not allow us to stage a peaceful *dharna* outside the CM residence.

However, let us continue the *dharna* at the residence of Deepak Damle. No one can stop us there. It is a small bungalow at Malabar Hill. Let us get as many wheelchair users as possible as it is very difficult to arrest a wheelchair user, a divyang, because the wheelchair will not be able to get inside the police van. The wheelchair, plus a divyang sitting in it, will be almost impossible to lift people with disabilities. The road is small and narrow, and we do not have to do anything to close the road. It will automatically happen. And if we get there by 5 p.m. and start our *dharna*, then by 6 p.m., we will be causing lots of problems for the Damle *parivar* (family) and his neighbours.

Social media comes in handy in these moments. Satya Prakash and Rajaram just put it on Twitter and Facebook that 15-20 wheelchair users were required for a cause like today morning. Polio survivors and amputee using crutches would also be required. A total of forty to fifty in numbers would do fine. Phone numbers of both my friends were splashed to get the address where we all were to assemble.

11 Ridge Road, Malabar Hills, was the official address of the commerce minister of the state, Deepak Damle. He lived here along with his wife and three children.

By 5 p.m., we had started our sit-in, and the megaphone had started to churn out the typical, cliched slogans.

"Deepak Damle hai hai. Tanashahi nahi chalegi, nahin chalegi (Death to Deepak Damle! Autocracy will not work! Will not work!)

Jo humse takrayga, mitti me mil jayega (Whoever collides with us will turn into dust.)

Humko barabari do! Hum bhi insaan hain (Grant us equality! We are humans, too!)

As we got into the *dharna*, the bungalow door opened. Damle's wife peeped out, wondering what all this commotion was about. When she saw that wheelchairs had virtually blocked the gate, she sent security to investigate. "Why are you shouting slogans on top of your voices?" Asked the security constable.

"We are protesting against the heavy-handedness and contemptuous way Damle had treated us in the morning at CM's residence." "But you have blocked the gate; how will anyone come in, and how will we go out?" Enquired Mrs. Damle. " Madam, we will seal the gate for about an hour. During this time, no one will be allowed to go in or go out." "How can you do this? Who are you? Shall l call the police?" One question after the other.

The main thing happening here was that the TV crews were assembling again. We had told them about this *dharna*, and they were more than happy to bring live news to their audience. Around this time, I got the disturbing news of our DUS protestor, who had been hospitalised as she became unconscious, had suffered a brain stroke, and was in a semi-paralytic state. Plus, DUS will again be the focus of attention of the nation. And Amrita, with a heavy bandage around her head, made for a very nice picture. It instantly connected the audience to the atrocity of the morning. Then cleverly, Amrita brought that into focus when the TV reporters interviewed her.

The slogans kept up the heat till the police came thundering in. They were well prepared this time. They had also called the fire brigade and were prepared to "flush" out the demonstrating DUS members. They were waiting for Minister Damle to come. It was not long before many spectators were also loitering around to see what *tamasha* (commotion) was happening. Damle came rushing in and barked, "You don't give up easily." He wanted the *dharna* to stop immediately or face the consequences. "You will not win. Can't you see the writing on the wall?"

Additional Commissioner Traffic had also arrived. He went straight to Damle and informed him that there was a traffic jam with cars piling up since this road had been closed to traffic. The situation was getting out of hand; he said, "We better do something fast because peak traffic will start in 30 minutes." Live coverage showed what was going on. Damle consulted Sr. Inspector on duty and urged him to take action as fast as possible. The fire brigade Sargent was also consulted. I could sense that things were heating up, and soon we would see action. I told my team to be careful now and be ready.

The police moved in first, but the DUS stuck to each other by tying a thick rope. It was difficult for the police to pick up the demonstrators, however hard they tried. The minister and the police ACP were getting frustrated and impatient as they could see the police were not making any headway. This became breaking news. *"Police manhandles disabled demonstrators"* was the main headline.

The fire brigade got a nod to start their operations and aimed the water hoses at the protestors, which included wheelchair users. My team got hit by high-velocity water cannons. The result was that apart from getting doused by the water, a few of my warriors, who were wheelchair users, fell in the melee. Some were shouting and screaming, and I realised our further stay here was untenable. Someone was bound to get seriously hurt. So, I yelled through the megaphone to stop the protest immediately. But it looked apparent that some of my team was injured due to the highhandedness of the police. In the meantime, a traffic police constable came rushing in and requested that the ACP come and see the traffic jam now as more than 100 cars had piled up right up to the door of the governor's house at Teen Batti. "Sir, the situation will get out of control in the next ten minutes. The cars and police/fire brigade vans and vehicles must be moved out from this road; otherwise, we will see cars spilling and piling up until the Chowpatty."

The injured included Satya Prakash Tiwari, a double amputee, who could not get out of the way when the police started pushing my team. His hands got trampled, and he had blood over his hands. I was furious when I saw Satya. I called all who had sustained injuries in the fight here to come forward and show their injuries to the TV cameras. Let the nation see how the police and an egoistic politician used their power to subdue, by sheer force, a handful of defenceless divyang in such a situation. One TV channel recording my interview asked me what my thinking was. Why was the administration so rough with my team and me?

"I think they are afraid of us. They do not know what to make of us. We are not political, and we are not a vote bank; we had no voice till we accepted that we were physically weak and vulnerable and formed the DUS. However, in the past two months, we made a name for ourselves by helping the two boys who were not permitted to use the college lift and the two visually impaired girls who got molested just because they could not afford to buy the Can of Distress Signals.

Now, of course, some young kids have been raped, plundered, and brutalised inside a government facility by the CM's wife's brother, and the wife is sheltering the perpetrator. We are being targeted because we are asking uneasy questions. This administration is corrupt and heavy-handed. Damle here has been at the forefront of hurting me as the commerce minister because we asked that women in this country be given the distress signals free of cost. He has threatened me by saying that we divyangs live at the mercy of our non-disabled brothers. And that we have no power or base. We are nothing. We will show such people how insulted we feel. Since independence day, the non-disabled have usurped our money and eaten into our resources. The nation has seen how Damle had stolen from us. We will show him how strong we are and how much power we have.

The police excess has resulted in Amrita being seriously injured, one girl is in hospital in a critical condition, and today there have been many injuries."

Damle, who had been seeing my interview inside his house, came out, snarled at me, and, pointing at me, said, "You are not going to get away from this nonsense. You are nothing; your DUS is nothing. You will be crushed." He turned and went inside the house.

I was seething with anger and shouted at him.

"Now that you have challenged me, I will show you tomorrow our power. You have not allowed us to protest; your police have injured and abused us. You will resign, and the CM will beg me to stop. The channels carried what had happened today. We have found a voice now. We will not be cowed down anymore. Everyone waited with bated breath to see what tomorrow would bring.

TWENTY-NINE

With one day remaining for the bye-election, we had a late-night meeting to discuss and finalise our program for tomorrow. I explained to them in detail what we would do and what would be the impact of our actions. "The police will be on alert tracking us all day tomorrow to ensure we are not up to any mischief. We require roughly 180/200 divyangs on wheelchairs, callipers, crutches, and visually impaired and deaf people. I explained to them what I had seen at our first exposure, where there had been a traffic jam within a few minutes of protestors gheraoed and some students spilling out on the street. In addition, today, in front of Damle's house on Malabar Hill, we had blocked that small road, 100 plus cars had been stuck in a jam in minutes.

Tomorrow at about 11 a.m. off, five of us will spread out in the city with 30-35 divyangs. Hamid will communicate with all of us and ensure that things are going smoothly.

No talking between our teams and smartphones were on the alert so that we could see what the TV was showing. We must have long ropes to make a ring so that if the police wanted to catch any divyang, they would have to pick up at least 25 of us. Each protestor must carry water bottles, and we had to be prepared to spend some time in the local jail. I knew what we were about to do was illegal and even a jailable offence, but what choice did we have? To be heard in this country, one had to be a nuisance or strong enough to make the authorities wake up and listen to our woes. In any case, we had some precedents to follow. There had been so many incidents in the past when a political party like Shiv Sena called the one-day city *bandh* (shut down), there was violence, looting, arson, and what have you, but the sitting authority did not take any action against the rioters.

In addition, I left it to Satya, Rajaram, and Ravin to work out the logistics, transport, and snacks to ensure things went smoothly. Moreover, yes, we had told all media about our intentions and the areas where we would hit. But no one knew exactly what we were up to. We did not want the news to leak out what was to happen; otherwise, the administration would have ensured that we did not do anything wild. The element of surprise had to be maintained. But no one could envisage the drastic action that would start in a few minutes.

The media will want to know why we are doing this, our demands, etc. The demands were simple:

1. Distress Signals Cans to be distributed free to all women of India.
2. All Direct Taxes against the divyangs are to be waived.
3. We demand that Kumud Salunkhe should be arrested immediately for helping her brother hide from the police.
4. We demand the immediate resignation of Commerce Minister Deepak Damle.
5. We request that up to 10 % of jobs be reserved for the divyangs.
6. Public toilets for people with disabilities should be on

every road.

7. All government buildings to have ramps built with immediate effect.
8. The government should pass a law that all buildings in the country must be wheelchair friendly.
9. We must have a ministry for people with disabilities with our minister in the cabinet.

Though in their favour, I must say that this government had made a movement to start a ministry for people with disabilities to call the Ministry of the Divyang, but it did not work out. The MLA from Amravati was to head this ministry.

We each had a copy of this and agreed to adhere to it.

By 10:45 in the morning, everything was in order. Our teams were placed at crucial spots, waiting for the clock to strike at 11 a.m.

At 11 a.m., the divyangs started pouring out of innocuous-looking Omni vans parked near their destination.

The first target was the traffic square of the Shivaji Chhatrapati Railway Station, the headquarters of the central railway. This was the main hub of local trains and upcountry trains leaving Mumbai. Daily some 5 lakh passengers use this station.

The traffic on the main square outside was enormous, going into at least a couple of lakhs of vehicles daily, maybe more. On pre-selected roads, Ravin's team of 30 DUS volunteers, wearing DUS T-shirts—spilt out of vans, with 15 of our team stopping the traffic on the road, going away from the station, and rest fifteen blocking the road coming into the station. They had a rope connecting all fifteen on either side.

The drama began.

Ditto was the scene at the Western Express highway where Rajaram and his team of 40 had stopped traffic on both sides of the highway at the toll *naka*.

Amrita controlled the Borivali station, where the vehicle traffic was enormous throughout the day. Amrita, with a bandage around her head, was striking figure again. Hamid and I were in charge of Haji Ali Square, which had enormous traffic. We blocked the road bringing traffic from Worli and the road from Peddar Road and Tardeo. We had 60 volunteers with us. Satya was in charge of all logistics. He had his non-disabled swimming trainees all over the protesting sites. He was constantly on the phone. Within 15 minutes, there was chaos, as cars were being stopped all over the city. The traffic was slowly coming to a standstill in many areas.

By 11.20 a.m., the police landlines were inundated with complaints from the general public. As the traffic started piling up, so did the street temperature, where the jam had a major effect.

We had ensured that school children did not suffer, so their buses, police, fire brigade vans, and ambulances were exempted from our strike. That is why the time of 11 a.m. was taken to start our protest.

TV reporters had a field day. It was major news, headlined, and breaking news on every channel. Was this going to be Gandhi revisited? No use of arms, no force, no violence, no animal hurt. The high command in Delhi started getting calls against the CM and the Commerce Minister Damle.

At 11:30 a.m., the joint Police Commissioner traffic approached us, urging us to halt our protest. "You are breaking the law and are being a nuisance. Please confer with your colleagues and withdraw in five minutes; otherwise, we will arrest you." We were in no mood to relent. We told him so. We were ready for anything, and just then, I got the report that the girl who had the brain stroke was getting better and had been shifted to the ward from the ICU. I sighed in relief and renewed our struggle with more vim and vigour. The media was all over, and live reportage was going on it. It was almost impossible for the police to take any action. We were aware of this.

Police officers had started arriving and taking their positions with an aggressive stance.

By 11:50 a.m., the CM was getting calls from the city gentry stuck in the jams. Calls from several highly influential people were inundating his office. People were cursing the administration, the protestors, and the police, as many would miss their flights, and some would miss their trains. Some had time-bound commitments, and the appointments must be readjusted and done later. The TV was blasting away with our demands and was interviewing men on the street for their views on our demands.

Akash Dangi said, who worked in the city as a helper and belonged to Sehore in Madhya Pradesh, "I agree with them and their demands... They are justified in asking for no direct tax on them as they spend a lot on their health and well—I also feel that free Distress Signal Can will help the women folk of the country and give them some security. It will give them lots of confidence to face life."

Sumit Sharma of Mathura was visiting the city to see some film shooting and have his fill of *bhelpuri*, his favourite snack. "I think that the DUS was a terrific organisation. They have made a dent in the political scene of this State in a very short time, and they have done the right things. No one was bothered about the handicapped people before. But now you understand the incredible trauma and challenges they face daily. At least in DUS, they have a movement that will take up their causes. So I agree with most of their demands."

However, for a businessman from Dharwar, Bhupesh Ashar, this whole thing was obnoxious. "I will a hundred per cent miss my flight to Chennai. These DUS guys must find some other way of protesting. This is criminal. They should be arrested. I sympathise with them and their cause, but who will pay for my air ticket and lost business?"

At noon, CM Ajit Salunkhe finally came to see the issues. By this time, more than 5,000 cars were stranded, and pressure was piling on the police and the government. The city had never seen anything like this before. Indeed, it wasn't easy to draw a parallel with anything like this in the world. Foreign news channels realised that something massive was going on here. Their TV crews had started reporting. Meanwhile, Google had closed the car navigation or the GPS since the cars were idling with nowhere to go.

However, DUS stayed put. The CM met us and demanded that we stop this nonsense. "What will you achieve by this? Holding a city to ransom is a criminal attack on the city. I will give you 5 minutes to reconsider; after that, police will move in and arrest you." He turned and left with the JT Commissioner. "Why cannot we move in and break this siege? Arrest them all. What is the problem? Get your act together. In 5 minutes, you start moving in. I have an election to run. Tomorrow is voting in the bye-election. How will this look? You better get your act together."

The JT Commissioner was perplexed; the protestors had all the sympathy, yet the CM did not understand the acute problem. How do I arrest the protestors? They are people with disabilities; it will not look good. National channels are showing this live. And also, this is slowly becoming an international issue, he thought.

Meanwhile, the cars stuck in the jams had crossed 10,000.

"Sir, DUS has cleverly kept the timing of 11 a.m. so that the school children are unaffected. They have also allowed ambulances, fire brigades, and police vans to go through—"Are you dumb wit, or what?" Snapped the CM. The ambulance can go through, but not the doctors. I have several calls from eminent doctors trapped in these godforsaken jams. They have operations lined up but cannot reach the hospitals."

There were some funny anecdotes as well. Ashutosh Bharadwaj, a keen dog lover, was travelling from Churchgate to his residence in Worli had got stuck on Peddar Road. He wanted to urinate badly. After two tough badminton games at his club, he had a milkshake and a bottle of mineral water. His two dogs, one Dalmatian, and the other a purebred black Labrador, were with him, and his man Friday was with them. The two dogs were his life; he adored them.

After about 90 minutes in the jam, he had a problem. He did not know what to do. At the same time, the dogs started whining slowly, indicating they also wanted to pee. They had been time trained, and their time had come. "Just wait," He told them softly, cooing to them. His dilemma was over, as he had no choice. He peed in the water bottle. But for the two adorable dogs, the waiting was getting too much. Dogs being dogs, they lifted their leg and let it go. The man Friday sitting with them in the back seat had to bear the entire brunt of the deadly smell.

The time was 12:30 pm, and the five-minute grace given by the CM ended.

The police constables, with canes in their hands, started to move toward the entrenched volunteers. The raids by the police on all the DUS protestors were carried on simultaneously at exactly 12.30 pm, and all raids were captured by TV crews from India and abroad.

The constables pushed the volunteers into one corner and started to lift them one by one. However, that was not possible as the thick rope came in the way. Lathi's charge was not considered, as that would be too brutal to comprehend. The JT Commissioner told his assistant to rush to the nearest hardware shop and purchase five of the biggest scissors on sale. While the salesman was wrapping and getting the warranty card, while that was being done, they came up with another idea. They would use tear gas to make the protestors leave the strike. The tear gas can be very nasty. However, the DUS was prepared for it, as Rajaram had told the team to carry a handkerchief. Moreover, if the police used teargas shells on them, they had to wet their handkerchief and put it over their face. That was it.

12:45 PM

The tension was building up with no respite from the jam. People were getting hungry and thirsty. Some wanted to go to the toilet but could do nothing about it. Satya and Rajaram told me in a conference call that let the non-disabled now know how it feels to be without toilet facilities. We have not had it for decades. The governments never realised how difficult it was for us. We had to retain our urine for hours.

Deepak Damle showed up on the order of the CM. The tear gas did not work at all. However, the scissors were handy as they easily cut across the heavy ropes. The order was given now to cut the ropes and start evicting the protestors individually physically. That was the biggest mistake by the administration.

By 1 pm, some 60,000 cars were stuck in jams. You could see them for kilometres. Chaos reigned all over. BBC, CNN, Fox News, Al Jazeera network, and many others lined up before me, wanting some answers. It was an impromptu press conference.

Q: What do you want to achieve from this action?

A: Respect, recognition. Nothing had been done for us since Independence in 1947.

Q: How long will you continue here? If the government accedes to a couple of your demands, will you call off the agitation?

A: As long as it takes to get an answer from this anti-people government.

This government has used violence against us. Not anymore. We will accept nothing less than an unconditional surrender from this government.

Q: What is the future of your party DUS if the demands are met?

A: It will be great. We will have our minister. In addition, for us, this is just the beginning. We are not interested in political power. However, if that is the only way forward, so be it. Our priority will always be to make life easier for the divyangs. Just then, a roar was heard, and all our attention was diverted to the source of that roar. Two women constables trying to lift a wheelchair user to the police van lost balance, and the wheelchair user came tumbling down, hitting her forehead on the pavement below. There was a howl from her.

The high command watching the TV reports was getting upset. They wanted to end this whole thing forthwith. The CM looked like a clown, not in control of the situation. The party got a bad name even abroad as the negative coverage continued unabated.

Ajit Salunkhe was not showing that he was disturbed but in turmoil inside. Outside, his visage showed a cool, calm, confident man as he watched the divyang woman fall and get injured.

He sent Damle to see if things were going smoothly and report to him immediately. The second accident happened just as Damle reached the spot. One of our volunteers, resisting pressure from two well-built policemen, jumped out of his wheelchair and landed on the ground with a thud trying to balance himself; he fell on his elbow, which suffered a fracture. He screamed with pain as Damle reached that spot and loudly enquired why it was taking so long to arrest these people.

The policeman in charge here looked flustered and explained that lifting a wheelchair with someone sitting in it was difficult. Ajit Salunkhe asked for more police officers to be deployed as hundreds of calls were being monitored from irate citizens who were very upset with the government. "Accepting their demands was the message they sent to thousands, thanks to social media. The CM contemplated what to do next when the high command called, with the PM himself on the line. "What is the problem, Ajit? You are making a mockery of our party. We claim to be following the ideals of Mahatma Gandhi, of non-violence, and here your police are hurting the handicapped, people with disabilities with no remorse. That joker in the pack, Damle, makes a fool of himself at every opportunity. Throw him out of the cabinet to start with—"

"But, Sir, there are some demands with great financial implications. I cannot take that decision alone." PM—"Send those demands to us we will debate over them, except the demand for Distress Signals." Then CM said, "DUS demands all women get free Distress Signals." Now sounding irate, the PM thundered, "Have you not heard what I said?" Moreover, he slammed the phone down. A flustered CM then called Damle and me to his side. He also called his security to get hold of a megaphone.

The time was 1:30 pm. Traffic police claimed that by now, there were effectively some 70,000 vehicles stranded. The Traffic Commissioner told him that some car owners could not control their urine problem and were emptying their stressed bladders on the roadside. It seemed that there was no end to the woes of the CM now. The Civil Aviation Minister had phoned the PMO and the home ministry about his problem.

“There are major problems at the Mumbai airport. As many passengers had reported, no flight had taken off for the past hour. The crowd is getting unbearable. The airport looks like a flea market, so cramped and populated. Nevertheless, the bigger problem I am facing is that since planes are not taking off, none are landing as no parking slots are available. Six planes are circling the airport in a holding fashion and are running out of fuel. It includes an Air India flight from New York in which the Minister of External Affairs is returning after attending the UNO general assembly session.

Eight more planes are coming in to land in the next 24 minutes. They all are getting low on fuel, especially our plane, with fuel left for only 33 minutes. I cannot divert them to any local airport yet. Nagpur and Pune airports do not have long runways. Ahmedabad is out since the president is going there to inaugurate the new Mahatma Gandhi Museum. So, that has been declared as a no-flying zone. The Air India Dreamliner will have to be diverted to Karachi. So, the situation is very serious and getting alarming every minute.”

With no revert from either the PMO or the home ministry, he phoned again within a minute, telling them that some 1,500 passengers were in danger, clearly showing his apprehension, fear, and urgency for action.

The PMO informed the Prime Minister, and he again got on the phone to talk to Salunkhe. There was chaos in the city, the financial capital of India. The PM was directly getting reports from different groups; the matter had to be resolved immediately. The country was already becoming a laughing stock in the international community.

“What is happening?” he barked.

“What is the delay?”

“We are doing it, Sir; we are getting there. I agree that the situation is not good for our party or us. But, Sir, unconditional surrender—”

“Do it,” said the PM. “Immediately; otherwise, keep your resignation ready, and we will have the cabinet secretary take over your burdens.” A flustered Ajit Salunkhe called Damle to his side and told him he was being sacked as a minister and had to resign immediately, no questions asked. He then announced that with immediate effect, Distress Signals were to be provided free of cost. And ministry for people with disabilities will be announced by the high command. Kumud Salunkhe will be arrested soon.

Regarding the tax cuts for divyang, he agreed that we should not be paying taxes, but this was not in his hands. However, he will recommend it and send it to the finance ministry at the centre. Trembling now and with a trembling voice that did not go over a whisker, he also said that the government was surrendering unconditionally. He then apologised to the people who suffered due to these roadblocks. He also announced that ramps would be compulsory in all upcoming buildings.

Then he beckoned me and asked me if I was satisfied. Then can you officially call off the protest? I thanked the CM and said I was satisfied with the outcome. I also apologised for any pain and suffering that may have occurred during our protest. My message went to Amrita, Hamid, Ravin, Rajaram, and Satya.

The protests were called off simultaneously from all areas we had targeted. It was a big victory for us. Now we must make use of what we have gained. I glanced at Damle, and he gave me a stare full of hatred. I had shown him the power of divyangs. Still, I stuck my hand out to him; no need to make an enemy for life. However, he simply turned away, his shoulders stooping as he slithered his way to his car. Gone was that arrogance, that smirk from his face. I remembered an Urdu *sher* which was very apt on Damle.

Na chal yahan tu sar utha utha ke,
Khizaan ne tujh se hazar chehere bigad daale bana bana ke

(Don't walk here with your head raised
Jealousy has spoiled thousands of faces with you)

As for me, I was happy that my community was at last recognised and will get what is due to them. My team met that night to celebrate a huge victory. We were inundated with calls from the media. Moreover, as expected, we won the bye-election the next day; DUS had arrived. Some media wondered why I was so quiet after gaining such a victory.

An Urdu couplet, which I liked a lot, came to mind.

"Keh raha tha shor-e-dariya se samundar ka sukoon,
Jis ka jitna zarf hai utna woh khamosh hai

(The river's raging is advised by the tranquil sea
The greater power you possess, the quieter you be)."

—NATIQ LAKHNAVI

As for me, I still hate the wheelchair, but I have reconciled with life; and I have also reconciled with my wheelchair. After all, there is not much I can do to change my destiny, so best to enjoy and live life king-size.

But the time had come to make very major decisions. How long could I depend upon Medini to be helping me? She had to have a life of her own. It would be criminal if I let her continue in the present mould. She should be free to carve out her future in her work with Star Sports or any other corporate she chooses to work in. I should not be a hindrance. What about Deepti? She does not deserve to have to be looking after me any longer. It has been almost four years since she was thrown into playing a role she was not accustomed to. Yet she hung on gamely and did what was required to keep me sane. Not one day she missed helping me.

I wish them well, but I have to decide what I must do.

~ The End ~

AN EYE-OPENER

My eyes cannot believe what I see in Vancouver, Canada, where I have come to rest and recuperate. Along with Deepti and Medini, we have landed here for a four months sojourn. Medini will return after three weeks for Mumbai since her leave can't be pushed beyond three weeks.

Vancouver is said to be the most accessible and disabled-friendly city in the world. And believe me, that it surely is.

There are ramps everywhere. And in every lift/elevator that I have used, the buttons to press where you want to go are really at the level of a wheelchair.

Every restaurant or dining place has got high tables where the wheelchair can easily enter so that you can eat the food aaram se (with ease).

Every traffic signal has protected crossings for the wheelchairs, which are battery-operated. People are extremely polite and willing to help you at the drop of a hat. Every public transport vehicle has a ramp down to the pavement level. And every washroom has a toilet, nice and clean to be used by people with disabilities only.

When we arrived at the Vancouver airport, we did not have to wait in the immigration or customs queue, as a ground staffer was there to guide us out of the airport and to the accessible parking area. Every parking facility must reserve 5 per cent parking bays for disabled patrons. If any non-disabled parks there, they will lose their license.

The family went to see a movie. Here too, some seats have to be accessible. Even if no one is from the differently-abled community, the reserved seats will go empty. No non-disabled person can use that area. No wonder Vancouver is considered the best city for the differently abled.

We in India, who have been unable to travel abroad, can't understand what I am talking about. And I am sure it will take us at least 5-6 years to get India to the level of Canada.

ACKNOWLEDGEMENTS

I must say that, yet again, I am indebted to the young and hard-working team of my publisher Inkfeathers.

I must include here the name of Uma Bokil, who had left the company to pursue her career in writing but not before she did the first editing of the book. I wish her the very best in her writing career.

Nonetheless, in place is another cool, calm, and highly helpful editor, Arya Koyal.

I also thank Yashika of Inkfeathers for bringing fresh ideas in marketing the book.

And, of course, the old guard of Sagar Kumar Bharadwaj and Anush Goel is very much there and always looking to scale new boundaries.

Starting with Match Point about a year back, this is the fourth book I am publishing with them, and I am delighted to be with them.

And though I have already mentioned the names of Arvind Prabhoo, Satya Prakash Tiwari, and Rajaram Ghag in my dedications, I still want to thank them for helping me so much.

They helped me to understand the major problems and trauma people with disabilities face every minute of their lives, which is the very core of this book.

I am indebted to all named above.

Also by Sanjay Sharma

Courage Beyond Compare: How Athletes Overcame Disability and Adversity to Become Champions

Pullela Gopichand: The World Beneath His Feat

Match Point: A Shuttler's Story

Mukti: The Salvation

Glory Beyond Dreams

MATCH POINT

A SHUTTLER'S STORY

SANJAY SHARMA

"Indian Badminton is better off today because there are people like him (Sanjay) who have devoted their entire lives to it." - SUNIL GAVASKAR

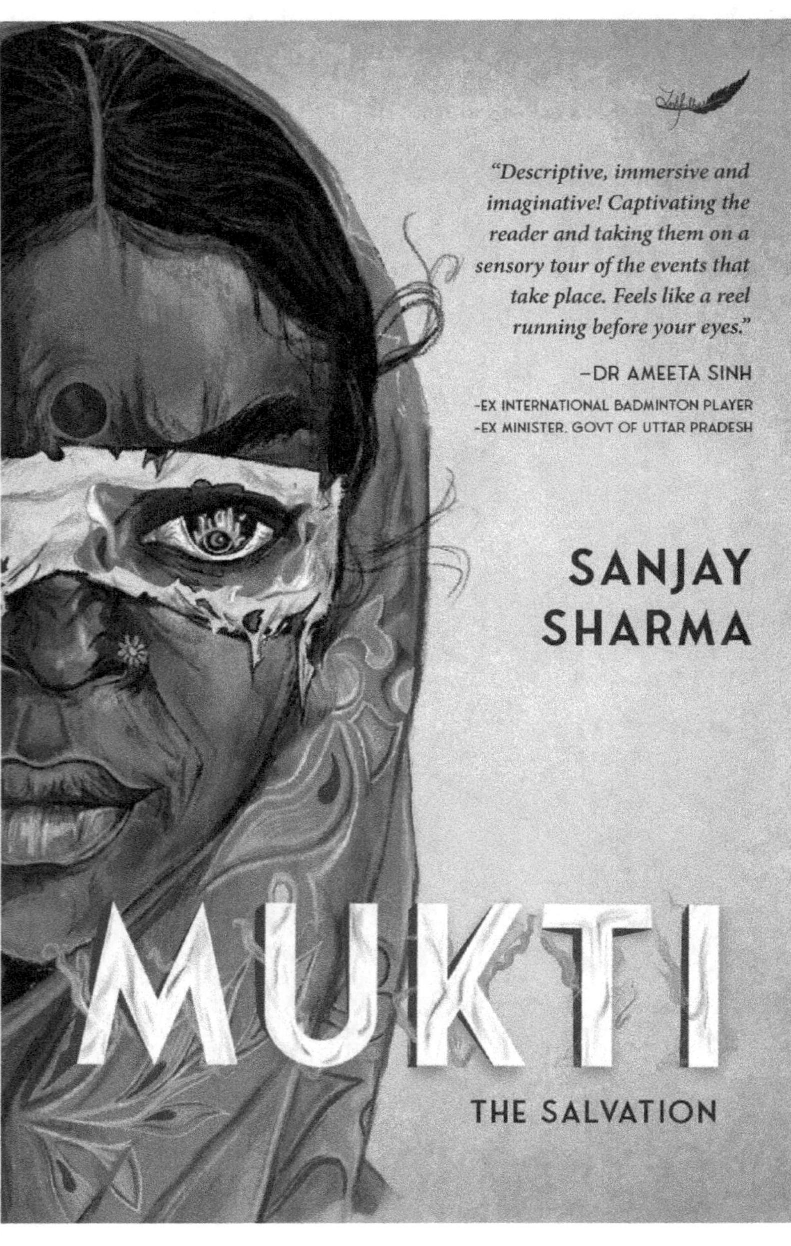
"Descriptive, immersive and imaginative! Captivating the reader and taking them on a sensory tour of the events that take place. Feels like a reel running before your eyes."
–DR AMEETA SINH
-EX INTERNATIONAL BADMINTON PLAYER
-EX MINISTER, GOVT OF UTTAR PRADESH
SANJAY SHARMA
MUKTI
THE SALVATION

SANJAY SHARMA

GLORY BEYOND DREAMS

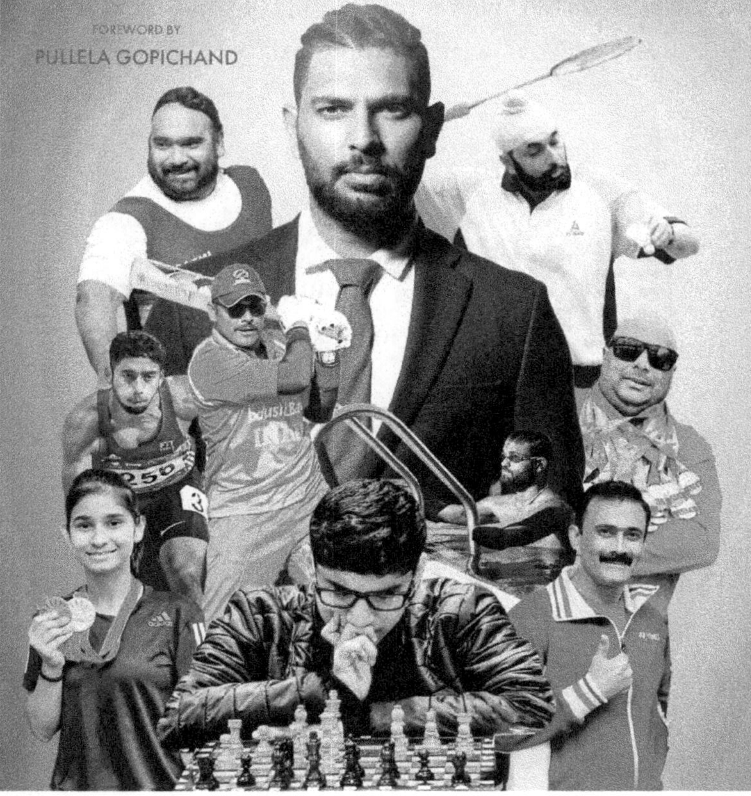

www.ingramcontent.com/pod-product-compliance
Lightning Source LLC
LaVergne TN
LVHW012055160826
845678LV00014B/2838

* 9 7 8 8 1 1 9 4 8 3 1 0 5 *